Embrace your true potential!

SCROLLS OF ZNDARIA

SCROLL 2
THE ALAMIST QUEEN

J.S. JAEGER

Illustrated by:
Jared Beckstrand

Illustrated by: Jared Beckstrand
Copyright © 2018
Jerry D. and Stephanie R. Jaeger

Synergy Books Publishing
www.synergy-books.com
PO Box 911232
St. George, UT 84791

All rights reserved. No part of this book may be reproduced or transmitted in any form or by any means, electronic or mechanical, including photocopying, recording, or by any information storage and retrieval system without written permission from the author, except for the inclusion of brief quotations in a review.

ISBN: 978-0-9885608-7-1 (Paperback)
ISBN: 978-0-9885608-8-8 (Hardcover)
ISBN: 978-0-9885608-9-5 (eBook)

Dedicated to Mandy, our real-life Cenaya, and to young women everywhere who overcome obstacles to achieve their true potential.

Acknowledgements

We are extremely grateful to all those who have helped make *The Alamist Queen* a reality.

Thank you, Jared Beckstrand, for once again beautifully bringing our world to life.

To our editors and beta readers: Caroll Shreeve, Summer Romney, Jenni Heiner, Rhea Racker, Jennifer Racker, and Rebekah White, thanks for helping us dot our i's and cross our t's.

Thank you, Dave Smith and Synergy Books Publishing for helping us create the finished product.

Special thanks to Mandy Jaeger for inspiring our Cenaya and providing invaluable feedback.

Chapters

#	Title	Page
1	A MOTHER'S LOVE	1
2	FIFTEEN	12
3	THE LAMP	22
4	KIDNAPPED	33
5	SHELLTOWN	43
6	DISCOVERY	53
7	THE CREATOR	61
8	THE FLETCHER	72
9	THE BEAST	82
10	THE CROSSROADS INN	93
11	RECOVERY	107
12	ESCAPE	120
13	PRINCE DAVIEN	136
14	A FATHER'S SECRET	150
15	THE GOLDEN WIZARD	164
16	THE HALLS OF MAGIC	177
17	RELEASE	186
18	EASTERN ISLAND	195
19	THE TROLL DUNGEON	209
20	UNLIKELY ALLIES	221
21	THE PRINCESS'S ARMY	239
22	THE WITCH'S HUT	253
23	THE LAIR	262
24	REUNION	272
25	REDRESS	283
26	THE FAIRIES	292
27	THE ALAMIST QUEEN	304

Chapter One

A MOTHER'S LOVE

Young Cenaya's eyes flew open. A bulky swamp creature stood over her bed. Thick leather armor covered its frog-like body. Her scream stuck in her throat. Moonlight beaming through Cenaya's open window shined off the grob's bulging, bloodshot eyes.

Run! Cenaya's mind screeched. Her five-year-old body didn't move.

The grob's forked tongue flicked through crooked, decaying teeth. Drool dripped past its thin, green lips onto Cenaya's nose and rolled down her cheek. The putrid smell made her stomach churn. Grabbing her by the neck, the grob lifted her away from her silky bed sheets.

Cenaya pulled at its slimy fingers. She couldn't breathe. Soft footsteps entered her room.

With a shriek, the creature released its grip. Cenaya fell to the ground and rolled away. The grob toppled over.

Cenaya felt a rush of relief. She recognized the arrow sticking out from the back of the grob's armor.

Cenaya's mother rushed to her side and stroked Cenaya's lavender hair. "My dearest! Are you hurt?"

Cenaya gulped for air. "No, mother." She could barely whisper.

Lifting Cenaya in her strong arms, her mother started toward the door. "The fortress is under attack. We must leave at once."

Cenaya buried her face in her mother's nightgown. Interlocking her fingers behind her mother's neck, Cenaya's arm brushed her quiver of arrows.

An explosion shook the fortress. They tumbled to the floor. Cenaya's ears rang. Her head throbbed.

Leaping to her feet, Cenaya's mother placed her quiver over Cenaya's shoulder. She flung Cenaya around onto her back. "Hold on tightly, my love." She darted out of the bedroom.

Cenaya clung to her mother's neck. Trembling with fear, she stared at one of her mother's pointed ears, trying to ignore everything around her.

Cenaya's mother bolted down the staircase. Cenaya felt as if she were flying. In the throne room, muffled shrieks and the sound of clanging metal drifted from the dining hall through the thick wooden door. She followed her mother's glance behind them. Fire danced halfway up the closest exit.

Cenaya's mother crept forward. "The dining hall is our only chance at escape."

Before they'd crossed the throne room, the battle sounds in the dining hall stopped. Her mother stood still. It remained quiet. She moved forward.

Suddenly, battle axes smashed through the door. Cenaya flinched. Three grobs charged toward them. She clung tighter to her mother's neck.

Her mother pulled three arrows from the quiver. Releasing one immediately after the other, she dropped all three grobs before they could advance. The dining hall remained silent.

Cenaya's mother stepped around one of the fallen grobs and peered inside the dining hall. Cenaya gasped. Many of the countless oak tables lay on their sides; several of them had been reduced to splinters. Dozens of motionless, bloody bodies—both elf soldiers and grobs—were strewn about the hall. Blood splatters stained banners stretching from the ceiling to the smooth wooden floor. Cenaya screamed inside. Tears burned her cheeks, but she couldn't look away. One of the heavy oak doors across the hall lay on the floor. The other dangled from its top hinge.

"Mother," Cenaya sobbed. "Why is this happening?"

"I don't know." Her eyes blazed. "I'll discover the truth once you're safe."

Cenaya's mother darted across the dining hall. A grob with a swamp hound stepped through the doorway. Her mother skidded to a stop in the middle of the room.

The grob's curly red hair flowed past her shoulders. Her eyes bulged but weren't bloodshot. A perfect redness emphasized her puckered lips. Her gown almost hid her distorted contours and matched her emerald-colored body.

She smirked, "What isssss thisssss?" The Swamp Witch's forked tongue vibrated. She pointed the python head on the top of her staff at Cenaya's mother. "Are you trying to essssscape, Queen Natalia?"

"Meredith!" Cenaya's mother gritted her teeth. "How dare you attack our kingdom! The Council will see you destroyed for this act of tyranny."

The hideous swamp hound growled and gnashed at them, pulling on the chain in Meredith's hand. Its stubby nose barely protruded from its flat face. Its eyes glowered. Slobber hung from its wide mouth. Cenaya shuddered.

Meredith hissed. It resembled sickening laughter. "You know ssssso little," she sneered. "Your Councccccil will sssssoon be dessssstroyed."

Several elite grobs dressed in chain mail armor strutted in, standing tall, crossbows readied.

Crackling sounds pulled Cenaya's eyes away from Meredith. Flames ate the wall behind them. "Mother!"

Her mother looked from Meredith to the wall. Cenaya trembled. They were trapped.

"Take usssss to the Alamissssst, and we'll let

your daughter live."

Cenaya's chest tightened.

"Never!" Cenaya's mother pulled an arrow from the quiver at Cenaya's shoulder. Before Cenaya could take a breath, her mother released the arrow, striking the remaining hinge on the double door. Meredith jumped to the side. The door slammed to the ground, flattening several grobs.

Cenaya's mother leapt from table to table until she reached the opposite wall. "Keep your grip sure," she instructed Cenaya.

Cenaya clasped her fingers together. Cupping her hands around her mother's glowing crystal pendant, she pressed them into her mother's chest.

Grasping a banner, Cenaya's mother pulled herself up, hand over hand. Cenaya tightened her hold. Twisting around, her mother dodged crossbow bolts fired by the grobs. She leapt onto a high window sill. Several more bolts bounced around them. One pegged into the log wall. She dove out of the fortress, catching a nearby bough. Just as it broke, she swung to a lower branch. Her agility almost calmed Cenaya's fear. She glided down several more branches until they landed safely on the ground.

Her mother kissed her forehead. Cenaya felt her love as if it flowed through her body. Her mother bounded into the forest, gripping Cenaya's arms tightly around her. Cenaya looked back at their home. Flames rose high into the night sky. Their mighty rosewood fortress crumbled. Tears dripped down her cheeks.

Branches snapped behind them. Something or someone was following them. Cenaya's heart leapt. "Mother!"

"I hear it."

Spinning around, her mother pulled an arrow from the quiver. The green-eyed swamp hound burst into view. She released the arrow, sinking it deep into the creature.

With a yelp, the hound skidded across the ground, leaving a rut several boot-lengths long.

Her mother turned to run but tumbled over with a groan. Cenaya rolled off her back. A grob flew overhead on a giant swampbat.

"What's wrong, Mother?" Cenaya cried.

Sitting up slowly, her mother winced. A bolt stuck out of her leg. "I'm afraid we must part. I need to get you away from here." She whispered a strange language as if to the woods. Turning back to Cenaya, tears filled her eyes. "I will join you as soon as I'm able."

"But, I can't leave you." Cenaya struggled to help her move to the cover of a nearby tree.

"If you stay, the witch will capture you. She will torture you until I give in to her demands. I cannot let that happen!"

Another batrider flew overhead. A bolt struck the ground near their tree.

Cenaya's lip trembled. "I don't understand, Mother. What do you want me to do?"

Her mother smiled lovingly and touched Cenaya's cheek. "I want you to be safe and happy." A red glow filled the forest. Her mother's shoulders seemed to relax. "Help has arrived." Transferring the quiver from Cenaya's shoulder to her own, she readied her bow. "The fairies will take you to your father."

"My father?" Cenaya gripped her mother's arm. "But he left us. I've never even met him."

Cenaya's mother released an arrow. A batrider fell from his swampbat, crashing into the trees below. Hundreds of rosewood fairies, each no bigger than her thumb, surrounded Cenaya.

She threw her arms around her mother's neck. "Why can't they take us both?"

Tears flowed down her mother's face. She hugged Cenaya and kissed her forehead once more. "I must give you time to escape. You are my world, my darling."

The fairies created a blanket beneath Cenaya. Raising her into the sky, they lifted her away from her mother.

"Wait!" Cenaya sobbed. "Come with me!"

Several more grobs charged toward her mother. She released several arrows and then turned to Cenaya. "Alatava lashay, my love!"

The fairies carried Cenaya further away. Several more grobs fell. More came.

"Mother!" Cenaya stretched out her arms as her mother disappeared from her sight. "I don't want to leave you!"

Cenaya buried her head in her arms, weeping as the fairies flew faster. Her mother's final words echoed in her head. *Alatava lashay*: the deepest expression of love in their language. She would always have her mother's love, but would she ever see her again?

Chapter Two

FIFTEEN

Cenaya stood atop the grand staircase. *I'm finally fifteen!* Her skin tingled. Her stomach fluttered with excitement. It wouldn't be winter outside for a couple of months, but inside, a magical whiteness draped the ballroom. Fluffy snowflakes drifted down from the high ceiling, vanishing when they reached the marble floor. Floating ice crystal lanterns painted waves of colored lights through the air. Children skated on a frozen lake with contraptions of leather and iron strapped to their feet.

A banquet stretched along the back wall. Silver apples, roasted dates, sugar figs, jelly tarts, fruit fritters, and berry puddings surrounded an assortment of meats—fried boar, skewered lamb, seared whale, salted eel, and smoked duck—arranged on the shell of a giant pearl crab. Everything but the meats made Cenaya's mouth water.

From a raised stage, six creatures with rabbit heads and halfling bodies filled the ballroom with symphonic music. Joyful chatter from countless guests dressed in their finest blended with the song. A table overflowed with a mountain of gifts. Everything celebrated her. Cenaya grinned.

A trumpet's signal silenced the crowd. All eyes turned to her. The band started a regal march. Stepping lightly, she descended the staircase. Her heart pounded. She didn't want to fall in front of everyone.

Prince Davien waited at the bottom. His

buttoned jacket and matching breeches traced his muscular figure. The cloak slung around his neck added to his charm. Locking eyes with him, her smile widened. His reassuring gaze relaxed her.

When she reached the bottom step, Prince Davien bowed before her. He lifted her under her arms and spun her around. Rainbows danced off her shimmering gown. He escorted her to the center of the ballroom. She couldn't take her eyes off him.

The band switched to an elegant melody. Prince Davien waltzed Cenaya around the floor, his every dance step flawless. His wavy blue hair swayed back and forth. She wished the song would never end.

The music slowed. Prince Davien dipped Cenaya over his arm. Raising her just as gently, he turned her toward the crowd and bowed once more. The onlookers responded with a chorus of adoring sighs.

The prince led her to a long line of guests

♦ The Alamist Queen ♦

who'd welcomed her as one of their own when her kingdom was destroyed just before her sixth birthday. Her heart swelled with appreciation for the kingdom of Taycod.

Bowing deeply, he kissed her hand. "Your admirers."

She giggled, then curtsied before a tigerman. His thick orange hair cascaded down his upper human body meeting the four legs of a tiger. The appearance of his people, the huminals, used to startle her, but now she admired their beauty. "Count, I'm honored by your attendance."

Cenaya embraced the countess beside him. Twisted into a bun, her spotted black and gold hair stood nearly a full boot-length above her head. An elaborate gown covered her half-human, half-leopard body. "My lady, you look as stunning as ever."

She continued down the line of royalty and nobility from Taycod and several other kingdoms. Taycod's wizard, Wynslow, an aged huminal with a goat's body and long beard, wished her much

♦ Scrolls of Zndaria ♦

success in the coming year. Another guest, a stunning woman with creamy skin, almond-shaped eyes, and straight black hair, encouraged Cenaya to be open to new opportunities for adventure and leadership. Cenaya greeted each guest graciously, never betraying that she'd rather be dancing with the prince.

The line ended at a beefy man with a well-trimmed beard and bushy blue hair. His gem-adorned crown matched his brilliant persona—rings on every finger, the finest silk clothing, and an extravagant sword at his side. Equally fantastic, though reserved and withdrawn, the queen sat directly below him. Pasty-skinned servants with deep red hair and red eyes, the race of all servants in Wishington, presented platters overflowing with food to the royal couple.

Cenaya curtsied before the thrones. She caught her father's gaze. As always, he stood in the shadows behind the king. She couldn't remember ever seeing him smile. Lavender hair flowing past his shoulders hid his pointed ears. A sleeveless golden breastplate emphasized his bulky biceps. Cenaya knew almost nothing about the duties he performed as King Tilus's chief commander.

King Tilus smiled and dismissed Cenaya with a wave of his hand.

She curtsied a final time, then rushed to an ice sculpture of three orcas jumping out of the water. Her dry throat ached. A different beverage shooting out of each orca's mouth landed in punch bowls on the table. She filled her glass with bluemelon juice and relished the cool relief.

"Cenaya!" A trio of voices called out behind her.

"Princesses!" Cenaya hugged all of them at once. Elizabeth, Victoria, and Abigail were three of the king's four daughters. They spent their days together being schooled on how to be proper princesses, and she adored them. "You three look gorgeous, as always."

"And you," Abigail sighed, "are almost old enough to marry."

♦ Scrolls of Zndaria ♦

Cenaya shook her head. "I'm not ready for marriage." She nodded at Prince Davien encircled by numerous females on the dance floor. "And I don't think your brother is either." Yes, she'd dreamed of marrying Prince Davien one day but didn't know if he felt the same devotion. He was only a year older than her and didn't seem ready for any long-term commitments.

"Oh, no." Victoria frowned at a girl coming their way. Her face looked chiseled from stone. Her stringy hair lay flat against her head. Her straight, dull dress was anything but fancy. "Look who's here to ruin the party."

The three princesses huffed, "Come on, Cenaya. Let's dance." Turning their noses up at their oldest sister, Kathlyn, they hurried onto the dance floor. Cenaya tried to follow them, but Kathlyn stepped in front of her.

"Happy birthday, Cenaya. I hope you are having a great time." She sounded sincere, but looked miserable.

"Why are you here, Kathlyn?" Cenaya stepped

around her. "You hate parties."

"I wouldn't miss your birthday," she said, laying her hand on Cenaya's shoulder, "even if it means supporting father's gluttony."

Her soft eyes reminded Cenaya of the love she'd felt from her over the years, but the way she constantly belittled her father and the royal ways wore on Cenaya. "I don't understand why you hate your father. You could have so much if you'd stop fighting him."

"Welcome, guests!" the king's voice boomed above the crowd.

The music and chatter stopped. Cenaya turned her back to Kathlyn. The king stood straight while floating in mid-air. Just as with any Djinn when they flew, a blue mist encircled his lower body. He spun around. The mist grew into a cyclone, creating a dazzling display. The crowd cheered. He stopped spinning, and the gentle blue vapor returned.

"Princess Cenaya!" he said. "We are awed by your beauty this evening." He landed beside

Cenaya. The mist vanished, and he took her by the hand. "In Wishington your wishes can come true! What wish do you desire today?"

Cenaya swallowed to remove the lump in her throat. She'd waited for this moment since she first learned the king granted a wish on an honored person's fifteenth birthday. She looked around at everyone who'd been so kind to her. "I wish my mother were here."

The crowd murmured.

Cenaya thought her father's eyes flickered.

The king's eyes grew big. "Your . . . mother?" He smiled gently and placed his arm around her shoulders. "My dear, that is a noble wish. I'm told there are those searching for your mother to restore her to power. But until that time, your sisters tell me of a different wish."

Cenaya blinked back tears. She missed her mother dearly. What other wish could she hope to receive? She looked at the three princesses and then grinned. "I wish I could fly like you and the other Djinn!"

King Tilus's smile filled his face. "Bring in the gift!"

The ballroom doors opened. A servant led in a white animal with a light-blue horn that matched the wings tucked against its body. Handing the reins to Cenaya, he bowed slightly.

"She is a cross between a pegasus and a unicorn." King Tilus lifted off the floor. "What will you name her?"

Looking in the magnificent creature's eyes, Cenaya stroked her mane. The animal nuzzled her neck. "I'll name her after my mother." Cenaya looked up at the king. "Her name is Talia."

Chapter Three

THE LAMP

"Cenaya!"

Cenaya cracked open her eyes to the excited voices of her princess sisters.

Elizabeth, Victoria, and Abigail jumped onto her oversized feather bed. "Cenaya! Wake up!"

Cenaya bounced slightly and pulled her quilt over her face. "Why are you excited to be awake?"

"Father's letting us go to the Lamp!" Abigail squealed.

"The Lamp?" Cenaya shot out of bed. That only happened a few times a year!

Rushing past a servant lighting the candles on her crystal chandelier, Cenaya smoothed her hair with a silver-plated brush, then secured it in a loose bun with an ornate clip. She splashed warm water on her face from the recently filled marble basin and dried it on a soft towel. Leading Victoria and Abigail into her closet, she stared at the walls of clothing surrounding her.

"I don't want to wear any of this!" she sighed.

Elizabeth joined them holding a simple, dull garb hanging out of its linen wrapping. "Why not wear Kathlyn's gift?" she smirked.

Victoria picked up the dress with her fingertips and threw it on the ground. "Why does she make these hideous things?"

"She wants everyone to look as ridiculous as she does," Elizabeth laughed.

Cenaya rolled her eyes but couldn't laugh. From the day she arrived in Taycod, Kathlyn had treated her with such love that she was the closest thing Cenaya had to a mother. Now she felt guilty every time she saw Kathlyn and tried to avoid her. "I have a better idea."

She hurried to a table overflowing with half-opened gifts from her birthday party several days earlier. Digging through the wrappings, she pulled out her gift from the countess: a blue dress with sparkling sapphire buttons. "This is perfect!"

Seated in Talia's custom-embroidered saddle, Cenaya flew between the princesses and the royal guards surrounded by their blue cyclones. She couldn't stop smiling. She'd always loved riding the few pegasi the kingdom kept for visitors, but now she had Talia. Stray strands of her hair fluttered in the wind. She drew in a deep breath of the crisp autumn air. Small birds screeched high-pitched greetings. Flying on Talia this morning made their unexpected trip even better.

The city of Wishington stretched along the coast. At its heart, the premium shopping center in Zndaria rose above its surroundings. From its slightly wider base, the Lamp curved upward to majestic flames. Sunlight glistening off the structure added to its aura of wealth.

They landed near the flames, and the mist around the Djinn disappeared. Handing Talia's reins to a servant, Cenaya followed the princesses through gold-plated doors into a white marble square chamber they called the cloud. Even with the guards, they had more than enough room to spread out.

A servant dressed in a brightly colored tunic stood in the corner next to a metal lever. He hardly lifted his head when they entered. "Greeting, princesses," he droned. "Which floor are you visiting first?"

"The Mermaid's Cove," Abigail insisted.

The servant pressed a button and pulled the lever. The cloud dropped slowly. Cenaya welcomed the flutters in her stomach. When it stopped, the doors opened to a watery paradise.

"Welcome, princesses!" A mermaid in a

sparkling pool splashed the water with her emerald tail. Small waves lapped against an island within the pool.

Leading Cenaya and the other princesses through a path created by the guards, Abigail paraded past a small crowd of huminals and olive-skinned peasants to a shop entrance that looked like an oversized clam.

"I won't like anything in here," Elizabeth huffed. "Pearls don't sparkle."

"We're not here for you. I owe Cenaya a birthday present." Abigail pulled Cenaya to a display of different colored pearl jewelry. "Pick anything you want."

Cenaya studied the rainbow in front of her but couldn't decide.

Abigail picked up a pearl necklace. "This matches your eyes." She clasped the necklace around Cenaya's neck and turned her to the mirror.

Cenaya's amethyst eyes appeared deeper than ever. An image flashed through her mind. "It's perfect." She stroked the necklace, lost in her thoughts. The pearls complemented her wind-blown lavender bun. For a brief moment, she felt as if she stared into the face of her mother. A tinge of sadness tugged at her.

"Well, if you're done here, follow me," Victoria ordered. "I want a treat."

Cenaya pushed the thoughts of her mother from her mind. Abigail motioned to a guard who approached the shopkeeper. They all followed Victoria out of the shop into the cloud.

"Take us to the Giant's Truffle," Victoria commanded without even looking in the servant's direction.

He pressed a button and pulled the lever. The doors opened at a higher level where the aroma of chocolateberries greeted them. Behind a long counter, an aged hill giant bustled in the oversized kitchen. Standing three heads taller than the princesses, her curls bounced against her shoulders as she collected ingredients and pulled delectable delights from the stone ovens.

Each princess piled her plate high with oversized truffles, bonbons, and fruit before drenching them in melted chocolateberrries. They followed Victoria to a table in the middle of the dining area. The guards stood at attention near the entrances.

Cenaya scooped up a bite of her truffle. It melted in her mouth. "I'm requesting this for my birthday party next year!" She dug in for some more.

Abigail swallowed a bite of her fruit. "Maybe Prince Davien will request it for his party next month." She lifted a bonbon with her fingers. "I promise, he'd do anything to make you happy." She grinned, wiping chocolateberry drippings from her mouth with her finger.

"Thank you for reminding me!" Cenaya shoved one more bite of her barely eaten treats into her mouth and stood up. She grinned at her sisters' questioning looks. "I need to get a gift for your brother while we're here."

"But I get to choose next!" Elizabeth whined.

♦ The Alamist Queen ♦

"We're going to the Boarian's Hut for mud baths. In fact, I'm done eating." She pushed away her nearly full plate. "Let's go now."

Leaving their plates of uneaten sweets on the table, they all joined Cenaya in the cloud.

"Back to the Mermaid's Cove," Cenaya instructed the servant. The doors opened once again at the familiar level. "Start without me." She stepped off with a guard right behind her. "I'll meet you there."

Cenaya rushed toward an entrance shaped like a skull. Light from within caused the eyes and mouth to glow. Passing a man in a deep purple robe and matching cap leaving, she stepped inside.

The shop carried anything one might need to go to sea. Stands held triangular hats folded upward toward the center, caps with stiff brims, and wide-brimmed hats. Swords, daggers, and black-powder pistols lined the walls. Tables displayed clothing for seamen and pirates alike. She felt certain the prince wouldn't appreciate any of it.

"May I help you with a purchase, Princess?"

Cenaya turned to the clerk behind her. "Yes, please. I'm looking for a gift for Prince Davien, but nothing I've seen is unique enough for him. Do you have anything else he would like?"

"Actually, I have just acquired the perfect item." Stepping behind the counter, he handed Cenaya a dagger. "It is the weapon of an Undead prince."

Crafted from black metal, the heel of the twisted handle held two emeralds embedded in a finely crafted face. Twisted crossguards rested against a fine scabbard. Cenaya pulled it out to reveal a curved dark blade sharpened on all sides.

"Surely such an item would be a worthy addition to Prince Davien's collection." He leaned over the counter. "I can let you have it today for ten gold bits."

Cenaya turned the magnificent weapon over in her hands. She couldn't imagine the prince owning anything like it.

"I'll even include this." The shopkeeper presented a leather sheath he pulled from a shelf.

Cenaya placed the dagger back in its scabbard and slid them both into the sheath. "I'll take it."

The guard escorting her completed the purchase. She strapped the dagger to her ankle, then rushed to the cloud. It opened several floors below to a wave of steam.

A hairy creature with a human body and the head of a boar greeted her. "Welcome, Princess." He handed her a robe and bathing suit. "Please come with me." Leading her to the changing rooms, he held the flap open and bowed once more.

Cenaya closed the flap to her hut, thrilled to be able to slip into the bubbling dark pools.

From behind, a hand covered her mouth. "I won't hurt you."

Cenaya knew that voice well. Pulling away, she turned to face the intruder. "Kathlyn!" she hissed. "What are you doing in here?"

"It is time for you to know the truth. Will you come willingly or do we have to force you?" Two bulky servants appeared through the back flap.

Cenaya's heart raced. Her eyes darted around, looking for the easiest way to escape. What would they do if she screamed? Bending forward, she reached for the dagger.

The servants lunged at her. One cupped his hand over her mouth and lifted her off the ground. The other grabbed her legs, removed the dagger, and handed it to Kathlyn. Kathlyn tucked it into her skirt.

Cenaya squirmed but couldn't break their hold. They carried her out the back of the hut into a dimly lit hallway. Panicking, Cenaya tried to kick the servant holding her legs. He tightened his grip.

Kathlyn looked at Cenaya with sadness in her eyes. "I'm sorry we're scaring you, but I'm doing this for your own good."

The servants placed Cenaya into a dark hole in the wall and let go.

Chapter Four

KIDNAPPED

Cenaya slid in the blackness. She tried to slow herself, but her hands skipped off a cold smooth surface. Her heart pounded. Dim light appeared beneath her. She shot out of the darkness with her legs and arms flailing. Landing with a thud in a huge cart, she looked around. Stained tablecloths and wet towels had broken her fall. Cringing, she jumped to her feet. She couldn't reach the top of the cart.

"Clear the way!" Kathlyn's yell echoed from the chute.

Cenaya moved to the side.

Kathlyn landed at her feet, laughing. "Thrilling, isn't it?"

"No!" Cenaya screamed. She hadn't seen Kathlyn laugh in years. Her anger stopped her from appreciating it. "You threw me down a laundry chute!"

"Calm yourself," Kathlyn sighed. "I'll help you out."

"I'm not going anywhere with you." Cenaya folded her arms.

"It's your choice," Kathlyn shrugged. The familiar mist encircled her feet.

Looking around at the grimy linens, Cenaya shuddered and grabbed Kathlyn's outstretched hand.

Rising above the cart, Cenaya felt her hair droop. Hot, humid air clung to her skin. She stared at a massive iron contraption filling a room larger than the castle's great hall. Sweat trickled down her face. Their only light came from flames pouring out the sides of the device.

"Where are we?"

Kathlyn landed near the contraption and dropped Cenaya's hand. "We're underground where the steamer powers the Lamp."

An awful grinding sound filled the air. Cenaya covered her ears. A monstrous chain pulled the cart she'd just been trapped in along a track away from the chute, replacing it with a second cart. A giant metal arm tipped the first cart over. Dirty laundry spilled out, splashing into an enormous basin that released a cloud of steam.

Cenaya clenched her fists. "I could have been killed!"

"But you weren't. Come with me." Kathlyn started toward metal stairs along the wall.

Cenaya wanted to rejoin the other princesses, but how would she find them? She sighed and followed Kathlyn.

The next level down, servants swarmed the steamer. Children transferred wet linens from it to women at washboards. After scrubbing them, they handed the linens to a different group of children who hung them on clotheslines. The constantly moving cable pulled the cleaned items back into the steamer. No one seemed to notice the princesses.

They reached a landing, but Kathlyn didn't stop.

"Must we really continue downward?" Cenaya snapped. "You need to take me back to the others."

Kathlyn looked back at Cenaya. "Keep your eyes open. You might learn something today."

On the next level, more pasty-skinned women and children took the now dried linens off the lines. After folding them, they placed them onto a moving leather belt that reentered the steamer, carrying the freshly cleaned laundry into the darkness above. One more level down, Cenaya watched with dismay. Servants of all ages pulled dirty dishes from the steamer's leather belts to be steamed and scrubbed and then reloaded onto

♦ The Alamist Queen ♦

the belt to once again be carried upward. None of the servants looked happy. They looked too thin and exhausted.

When the stairs ended on the next level, Cenaya gasped.

Hundreds of male servants dressed only in wool shorts circled the steamer. Flames covered their arms and shot out of their hands. The fire entered the steamer through hundreds of open doors. Stifling heat mixed with the already overpowering humidity.

Cenaya gaped. "How are they doing that?"

"Just like the Djinn control air, Efreet genies conjure fire."

"But I haven't seen that before. My servants use flint to light my candles."

"They're only allowed to use their powers to run the Lamp. If they're caught using them anywhere else, they're punished with death." Kathlyn pinched her lips together.

"Who would kill them for that?"

"My father."

♦ Scrolls of Zndaria ♦

They stood in silence watching the Efreet a moment longer. Cenaya marveled at the beauty of their flames. The thought of them being killed just for using their powers made her sick.

Kathlyn started forward again. "When the Djinn won the Genie Wars, my grandfather enslaved the Efreet. We could now coexist peacefully if given the chance, but the kingdom has become reliant on the servants. My father is a lazy man. He restricts the use of their power so he can keep them as slaves."

The princesses stopped in front of two metal doors. When they opened, several Efreet men exited a metal box and walked toward the base of the steamer.

One of them smiled at Kathlyn. "Haze is waiting for you."

"Haze?" Cenaya looked to Kathlyn for an explanation.

Without a word, Kathlyn stepped inside and pulled the doors shut behind them. A simple torch provided light. The heat lessened slightly.

Standing shoulder to shoulder, Cenaya and Kathlyn could reach out and touch the walls.

"This is the servants' cloud." Gripping a thick rope, Kathlyn started pulling hand over hand to raise the box. "Have you ever seen a servant other than the operator inside the main cloud?"

Cenaya didn't want to admit she hadn't. The box rose slowly, no stomach flutters, no sudden jerks. Kathlyn raised them smoothly, all the while explaining more mistreatment of the servants to Cenaya. She challenged her to watch how neither the king nor any of the royal family ever looked the servants in the eye, how they were only spoken to when given a command, or the harsh reactions they received for simple mistakes.

Cenaya listened intently. None of that seemed right, yet she hadn't noticed it. Could Kathlyn be making it up, or had Cenaya really been that oblivious to the mistreatment of others?

The box clinked to a stop, and Kathlyn secured the rope. The doors opened to a dusty, dank stable and the strong scent of manure. The stalls held numerous different animals—from horses to camels, bears to giant lizards.

An Efreeti young man slightly taller than Kathlyn approached them. His wavy bright-red hair fell to his shoulders. Cenaya couldn't place how she knew him. He scooped up Kathlyn and spun her around. Pulling her into him, he pressed his lips to hers and spun her around again. Their hair—his red and hers blue—created a breathtaking contrast.

Cenaya's jaw dropped.

He steadied Kathlyn on her feet. She turned to Cenaya, grinning from ear to ear. "Cenaya, this is Haze, my fiancé."

Cenaya looked from Kathlyn to Haze and back to Kathlyn, dumbfounded. "But you're betrothed."

Kathlyn locked eyes with Haze. "Yes, but this is the man I love and will marry." Kathlyn pulled a handful of gems from her pocket. "I brought some more."

Haze put them in his pocket, then stroked her hair. "You're incredible. This should give us enough."

Cenaya stared. Her eyebrows scrunched. If the couple noticed, they didn't respond.

Haze led them to a barrel-filled wagon hitched up to four old mules. Their rib cages pressed on their hides. Their eyes drooped.

Haze bowed to the princesses. "Your chariot awaits."

Cenaya started for the seat. Kathlyn reached out to her. "We need to hide in the back."

Cenaya stepped to the rear of the wagon. First, Kathlyn had kidnapped her. Now, she wanted her to hide. Cenaya looked around. Should she try to escape? Could she run fast enough to get away?

Kathlyn climbed into the wagon. "We need to get outside the city walls. I'm sure the guards are looking for you by now." She held her hand out to Cenaya. "I know I haven't given you any reason to trust me today, but please do. I think it's important for you to see a different side of Wishington."

Cenaya searched Kathlyn's eyes. She only saw love, no malice. Curiosity overpowered her feelings of concern. Grabbing Kathlyn's hand, she pulled herself up and settled between the smelly barrels as Haze threw a tarp over the wagon bed.

Chapter Five

SHELLTOWN

Blinded by darkness, Cenaya tried to identify sounds. The mules' hooves clomped. The wooden wagon squeaked. Drifting laughter reminded Cenaya of when she played as a child.

The wagon shuddered to a stop.

"What's in the wagon?" a harsh voice demanded.

Haze's calm, deep voice replied, "Breakfast scraps from the Lamp for the waste."

♦ Scrolls of Zndaria ♦

A sliver of light broke through the darkness, most likely a guard confirming Haze's story.

"Move along," the voice said.

With the slap of leather, the wagon moved again. Cenaya realized she'd been holding her breath and exhaled. This time, other than the sounds of the wagon and mules, she only heard silence. Why would they take her to the waste? The longer they rode, the more thoughts plagued her. How would her father react when he learned she'd disappeared? What consequences would Kathlyn face?

Finally, the wagon stopped a second time. Light flooded the wagon bed, and Cenaya squinted at the blinding sun. Jumping to her feet, Kathlyn helped Cenaya up.

Cenaya couldn't have prepared herself for what she saw. They'd brought her to a village, not the waste. Hundreds of small huts built from giant pearl crab shells surrounded them.

Haze blew a conch shell twice, then turned to Cenaya. "Welcome to Shelltown."

♦ The Alamist Queen ♦

Hundreds of Efreet swarmed out of the huts. Women, children, and old men each carried a pearl crab shell to the wagon. Kathlyn pried the tops off the barrels and picked up a wooden ladle. Cenaya also picked one up. Peering inside the barrel, she was shocked. They may not have gone to the waste, but the barrels *were* full of breakfast scraps mixed together. Haze and two other Efreet joined Kathlyn and Cenaya, and they proceeded to fill the shells of the Efreet with slop from the Lamp.

Feeling out of place in her dazzling clothing, Cenaya worked in awe. The Efreet reacted to what she saw as garbage with extreme gratefulness. Not one complained or grumbled. A half-eaten chocolate truffle caught Cenaya's eye. She felt sick remembering how much food she and the princesses had wasted that morning.

The line ended with a very thin lady with pale skin and grey-streaked red hair. She rested an extra-large shell on the side of the wagon. Haze and Kathlyn filled it as high as possible.

Kathlyn laid her hand on Cenaya's shoulder. "Cenaya, will you help Isabel carry her food home?"

"Definitely!" Climbing down from the wagon, Cenaya lifted one side of the shell. "Which way do we go?"

"I'm this way." She nodded over her shoulder. "Thank you." Her tired eyes confirmed her gratitude. She sounded much younger than she looked.

They made their way past numerous huts until they neared a doorway covered by a leather cloth.

"Mayah, I've returned," Isabel called out.

A small hand moved the cloth.

Inside, Cenaya helped set the food on the sagging wooden table next to several well-worn plates. A plain wax candle provided light for the single room. The only additional furnishings of the home consisted of a simple iron stove, several hay beds, and a rug woven from mismatched fabric.

♦ The Alamist Queen ♦

From behind the leather cloth, a young girl rushed to Isabel. The older woman bent down to the level of the girl's sparkling red eyes. Wrapping her arms around her, she rubbed her nose to the girl's petite, freckled nose.

The young girl giggled. "Thank you for the food, Mother! I found this for you." She pulled an oak leaf from her pocket. "I couldn't find any flowers but wanted you to have something to wear in your hair." She tucked the leaf behind her mother's ear and kissed her cheek.

Cenaya used to place flowers in her mother's bun. She blinked back tears. *Stop it, Cenaya!* She scolded herself. She always missed her mother, but she hadn't cried about it in some time. Why were today's memories hitting her stronger than usual?

"Who have you brought home with you, Mother?" Mayah turned to Cenaya and smiled.

Cenaya's heart sunk. Her mouth fell open, but she quickly closed it. Draped by stringy red hair, dark spots covered the swollen other half of

Mayah's face. Her eye bulged from its socket. Her puffy lips revealed the lack of teeth.

"I scare people," Mayah said without even flinching.

"Oh, no, sweetheart!" Cenaya rushed to her. "You're wonderful just the way you are!" She stroked her deformed cheek and brushed the hair out of her eye. "Does it hurt?"

"Yes, especially when I eat," Mayah shrugged. "But, I'm used to it."

Cenaya looked up at Isabel. "Can't the healers do something?"

Tears filled the woman's eyes. "Most healers won't treat the Efreet, and we can't afford to pay those who will."

"You don't have to worry about me," Mayah insisted, turning Cenaya's face back to her. "There's bigger problems in Shelltown than this."

Cenaya pulled her close. This precious child sounded so grown up. She shouldn't have to suffer. In the distance, Cenaya heard yelling and banging outside. She turned toward the door.

"Did you hear that?"

Mayah's mother furrowed her eyebrows. "I don't hear anything."

That didn't surprise Cenaya. Her sensitive elf hearing often allowed her to hear things others couldn't. "Stay inside. I'll find out what's happening."

Darting outside, she ran toward the commotion. Around a hill, numerous young olive-skinned peasants and huminals taunted several Efreet families, challenging them to show their power. A young man smashed a hut with a club, reducing it to shards.

Cenaya sprinted to the group. "Stop it!"

The bullies turned to her. A boy with the lower body of a wolf tapped his club in his hand. A half-lion young lady and an olive-skinned young woman stepped up behind him. Both swung their clubs and sneered. Cenaya looked around for something to use as a weapon. She didn't like her options.

The wolf boy jeered, "And I suppose you're

going to stop us all by yourself?"

"We'll stop you!"

Cenaya looked behind her, relieved to see Haze, Kathlyn, and Haze's other friends there to help.

"Leave our town and don't come back," Haze demanded.

"Please, use your powers to stop us," the wolf boy laughed. "I'll be the one to report you to the king so I can watch your execution."

Haze charged, ripping the club from the wolf boy's hand. Rearing up on his hind legs, the wolf boy kicked Haze in the gut. Haze doubled over and fell to his knees.

The young woman grabbed Cenaya around the waist. Wrestling her to the ground, she elbowed Cenaya in the side of her head. Cenaya pulled her knees to her chest and kicked the girl away. She got to her feet just to be knocked face-first back to the ground. Struggling to breathe under a great weight, she strained her neck to see behind her. The lion girl stood on Cenaya's shoulders and legs. She couldn't free herself. Her new pearl necklace pressed painfully into her chest.

"Enough!" Kathlyn yelled from within a cyclone above the fight. Debris from the shattered homes flew through the air. Her face shone more beautifully than ever. She shot a powerful gust of wind from her hands. The lion girl crumpled into a heap at Cenaya's side.

Staying low, Cenaya covered her head with her arms.

Another blast of wind separated a pack of olive-skinned young men, throwing them to the ground. Haze stood from beneath the pile and blew Kathlyn a kiss.

"The guards are coming!" the wolf boy said. "We'll finish this another day." He bolted away with the others right behind him.

Haze helped Cenaya to her feet.

Kathlyn landed beside them. Her eyes darted around. "We have to go before the guards catch us."

"I can't leave yet." Cenaya ran into the village,

pretending not to hear Kathlyn's protest. She rushed into Mayah's hut, removed her necklace, and placed it in Mayah's mother's hands. "Sell this, and take Mayah to the healers."

"But," Isabel gasped, "I can never repay you for this."

"I don't want to be repaid." She squeezed Isabel's hand. "I want to help Mayah." She bent down and kissed Mayah's deformed cheek.

Mayah wrapped her arms around her neck. "Thank you," she whispered. "You're my angel."

Cenaya couldn't remember the last time she felt this happy. She stroked Mayah's hair. "I have to go, but I will see you again." She hugged Mayah once more. She had to find Kathlyn and explain.

Stepping outside, Cenaya's smile disappeared. She found Kathlyn, hovering above the hut, surrounded by ten stern-faced Djinn guards.

Chapter Six

DISCOVERY

"You took Cenaya to Shelltown?" King Tilus stood in front of Kathlyn, shaking with rage. The queen sat in her throne, staring at the floor. Cenaya's father stood next to the king's throne, his face unreadable. "That place is forbidden!" The king raised his hand toward Kathlyn, then dropped it away from her.

Cenaya winced. She'd never seen the king this angry.

♦ Scrolls of Zndaria ♦

Standing firmly, yet at ease, Kathlyn responded calmly, "Why are you afraid of Cenaya learning the truth?"

King Tilus glared at her. Cenaya held her breath. Would he strike her? The king sat back in his throne and scowled at Kathlyn. "The truth is that the Efreet serve the kingdom in exchange for their protection, as they have since the treaty of the Genie Wars. For your defiance, you are confined to your room. Be gone from my sight!" He flicked his wrist in the air.

Kathlyn placed her hand on Cenaya's shoulder. Her face remained still, but her eyes seemed to smile. She nodded, then walked out of the throne room without looking back.

Cenaya stood silently in front of the king, waiting to be addressed.

"Cenaya." The king's demeanor had softened. He sounded tired. "I'm sorry you had to witness that horrible place. Kathlyn should never have taken you there."

"Your Majesty," Cenaya spoke as timidly as

she felt. "Why is there such great poverty in Shelltown when your kingdom has so much wealth?"

"I don't expect you to understand, my dear. Peace in this kingdom comes at a cost. It is as it must be."

"But . . ."

The king raised his eyebrow at her. His stern face challenged her to say more.

Bowing, Cenaya held back her thoughts. "My apologies, Your Majesty."

"You'll make a great queen someday." The king grinned.

A shiver ran through Cenaya.

He waved as if he were bored. "You're excused."

Stepping around the throne, her father escorted her from the throne room.

As usual, she couldn't read the expression on his face. "Are you angry with me, Father?"

"You're now old enough to discover the truth, but you must use discretion in your search." His response didn't answer her question. "Right now, you must come with me." They turned down a lengthy hallway filled with portraits of the royal ancestors.

She stole glances at her father. Where was he taking her? He seemed more stiff than usual, if that were possible.

He slowed his walk. "My Princess, do you know of something called the Alamist?"

"It sounds familiar." She shrugged. "But I don't know why."

"Did your mother ever take you into the stony mountains above the fortress?"

Cenaya thought briefly. "Yes. We walked through a dark cavern until we came to a massive milky stone wall. It came alive when Mother touched it." Cenaya smiled at the memory. "It was amazing. She asked it questions, and it showed her the answers. She showed me marvelous places in Zndaria and said we'd visit them some day. She allowed me to ask it anything." Cenaya paused and looked at her father. "I . . . I asked it

♦ The Alamist Queen ♦

to show me . . . you."

He looked surprised. "And?"

"You were crying." Cenaya gazed at her father tenderly. "That's all I remember."

He looked touched for a moment, but then his stiffness returned. "The milky wall is the great seer stone known as the Alamist. In the ancient elf tongue, it means *the all knowing.* Unlike smaller seer stones, nothing is hidden from its view. Even the most powerful magic cannot block it." Her father stopped and gripped her shoulders. He stared into her eyes. "The army that controls the Alamist will always have the advantage. It will know everything about its enemies, nothing hidden, no surprises."

Cenaya swallowed hard, frightened by his sudden intensity. "Why . . . why are you telling me this?"

"Someday, you'll become the Alamist Queen, the one ordained to wield the power of the Alamist." Clearing his throat, he started down the hallway and spoke matter-of-factly, "I'm taking

♦ Scrolls of Zndaria ♦

you to meet a man I've served for many years." He motioned to a full-length painting at the end of the hallway. The portrait depicted a clean-shaven, handsome man with short dark hair and steely eyes. Tall and muscular, his leather vest draped down to his thighs over his silky shirt and dark grey sash. "He calls himself the Creator and plans to use the Alamist to further his designs throughout Zndaria."

Stopping at the painting, Cenaya glanced down. Her dress showed signs of her adventure in Shelltown. She rubbed off dust and bits of food until she felt mostly presentable again. Her father chanted. Cenaya knew several languages but didn't understand this one. He took her hand, and they stepped through the painting into a hidden corridor.

Stunned, Cenaya followed her father down a tight spiral staircase lit by a few wall-mounted torches. She wanted to stop, to try to make sense of everything. His quickened pace told her that wasn't an option. Hurrying to keep up with him, her mind raced. Why was there a secret part of the castle? Who else knew about it? Did anyone else know about the Creator?

They entered a simple, dingy room where several Djinn guards faced a tall red mirror. Their eyes followed Cenaya and her father. Grasping her hand once more, he touched the mirror. It began to shimmer. They stepped through the mirror into a room of black rock walls, and Cenaya's skin tingled.

Rust-skinned monsters with bulky legs and barbed tails jumped to attention next to a metal door with no handle. Cenaya stayed close to her father. A shadow moved across the door. She looked closer. The shadow—a ghostly creature with piercing red eyes—nodded to her father before turning and passing through the metal. The door swung open to a long hallway of the same black rocks. The shadow allowed them to pass, and the door closed behind them.

Cenaya shuddered. "What was that thing?"

"The shadow warrior is the Creator's greatest

scout." They moved down the hallway. "It blends in with the shadows and can easily remain undetected. It's one of the many methods the Creator uses to advance his armies throughout Zndaria."

Cenaya took a deep breath. From Shelltown to hidden corridors in the castle, she'd discovered more about Wishington today than she had since she arrived. And now she had to meet this man her father called the Creator.

Chapter Seven

THE CREATOR

At the end of the hallway, Cenaya and her father entered a room larger than King Tilus's ballroom. Bronze statues and marble busts perched on granite pedestals stood between fine paintings. Flames spun in a dazzling display in the center of the room.

A woman with long black hair draped over her striking red robe and a man in tattered clothing stood beside a table bearing a feast. The man

♦ Scrolls of Zndaria ♦

Cenaya saw in the portrait sat on a throne beside a table holding a large, elegantly wrapped gift. He disappeared from the throne, reappearing next to Cenaya and her father.

"It's a pleasure to finally meet you, Princess." He kissed her hand.

Cenaya curtsied. He looked exactly like his painting. Her stomach fluttered despite an odd feeling she couldn't identify.

"I'm grateful Kevic is finally introducing us."

Cenaya hadn't heard her father called by his name in years. She called him Father. Everyone else in Taycod simply called him the chief commander.

"I brought her after she turned fifteen, just as I promised."

"Yes, you did." The Creator placed his hand on her elbow. "Cenaya, my dear, I couldn't make it to your birthday party, but I have a gift I wanted to give you personally." He led her to his throne. Her father joined the others but watched her closely. Sitting back on his throne, the Creator gestured to the package. "This was made especially for you. Please, open it."

Lifting the lid, she pulled out sleeveless golden armor that matched her father's. The thin, flexible metal felt more exquisite than anything she owned. "It's beautiful!"

"I'm glad you like it," the Creator smiled. "This impenetrable breastplate is magically woven quirillium. Let's see how it fits." He clapped his hands.

In an instant, she wore the armor over her dress. It fit perfectly. "How did you do that?" she gasped. "Are you a wizard?"

"Oh, I'm much more than a wizard." The Creator grinned. "When you join me, you'll have everything your heart desires. Extravagant clothing." He twisted his hand in the air. A shimmering ball gown draped over his hand. "The finest jewelry." Once again, he rolled his hand. The gown vanished, and a diamond filled his open palm. With another wave, it disappeared. He locked eyes with Cenaya. "I can give you anything you imagine."

Cenaya stepped back, breaking his stare.

"Cenaya, my dear." The Creator stood up and placed his hand on her shoulder. "I'm creating a better world. One where people escape suffering and have everything they need. Don't you agree that would be a better life for your new friends in Shelltown?"

"How did you know I was in Shelltown?"

"I saw you there in my seer stone." He gestured to a table encasing a milky stone as if she'd asked an unnecessary question. "The compassion you showed that little girl confirms I need you on my side."

He seemed to know a lot about her, maybe too much. "Why do you need *me*?" She replaced the lid on her gift. "I'm only fifteen years old."

"I need the Alamist. Next year, you'll be of age to control it. With that power, I can stop my blood-thirsty enemies who oppose peace throughout Zndaria. I can ensure your compassion is spread to everyone who is willing

♦ The Alamist Queen ♦

to join me. I can make everyone—including little Mayah—happy."

She stared at the box instead of looking at him. "My mother is the queen, not me."

"Yes, but unfortunately the Swamp Witch refuses to communicate with anyone outside her land since the attack on your home, and we've been unable to locate your mother."

Cenaya looked from her father to the Creator. "That's what my father has told me. But, that doesn't mean she's gone."

"Of course not. But, it does mean we must be prepared." He touched her elbow again. "Come with me, my dear."

Cenaya looked to her father. He nodded his approval.

The Creator led her out onto a dark-red rock balcony of the castle. The scene in front of her felt like a beautiful nightmare. Glowing red and black pillars jutted up from the ground. Black mountains towered around them. Magma flowed down the mountains, spilling into a shimmering red lake, illuminating the darkness overhead.

She had never seen anything like it. "What is this place?"

"This is the underworld."

A dragon flew down to hover directly in front of her. Cenaya ducked behind the Creator. He pulled her in front of him, face to face with the dragon. Its molten scales rippled. It thrashed its spiked lava tail. She felt tiny beside its massive head. She gaped into its enormous eyes and felt the heat of the flames engulfing its insides. Steam billowed from its nostrils.

"You're perfectly safe," the Creator said. "The Lord Dragon is under my control."

The dragon snorted. A gust of wind blew through Cenaya's hair. Her knees buckled, and she grabbed the edge of the balcony. The dragon flew away to join numerous others circling above a sea of rust-skinned creatures.

"When the time is right, we'll advance against Meredith and rescue your mother, if she is still alive. Once we have control of the Alamist, whether with you or your mother as queen, my army will ensure peace for all who desire it."

Cenaya looked over the valley. How could such a terrifying army bring peace?

"In addition to my magnificent army, I have members of my Court to aid and advise me." The Creator turned her back to the castle. "They're waiting to meet you."

Cenaya followed the Creator back into the throne room. In addition to the two people who'd been waiting with him before, two more individuals had joined her father. All five of them strode toward the Creator.

"Cenaya, my dear, this is my Court." He put his arm around her shoulders and moved her forward. "This is Cenaya, Kevic's beautiful daughter and the future Alamist Queen."

The man in the tattered robe took her hand in his. A disorderly combination of colors streaked his disheveled hair. Numerous hues speckled his eyes. His robe hung over ratty clothing. "We're honored to meet you." He kissed her hand.

♦ Scrolls of Zndaria ♦

The Creator dropped his arm from Cenaya's shoulders. "The Infinite Wizard is the greatest wizard of all time."

"I'm pleased to meet you." Cenaya curtsied. He didn't look powerful. He looked confused and disorderly.

He stepped back and allowed the woman to come forward. Her black hair cascaded down the back of her brilliant, sashed robe. Cenaya recognized her from her birthday party.

The Creator continued his introductions. "Empress Zhen preserves magical creatures for our efforts."

"Did you enjoy your birthday gift, Princess Cenaya?" Empress Zhen spoke the common tongue correctly but seemed to think about every word she spoke.

"Yes! Talia is wonderful!"

"I'm glad you like her." Empress Zhen smiled. "She is from my land and one of the last of her kind. A beautiful gift for a beautiful princess." She bowed to Cenaya.

"Thank you." Cenaya bowed in return. "You're very sweet."

"We look forward to you joining the Creator's Court, Princess." A voice rattled from behind Empress Zhen, who bowed to Cenaya once more, then stepped aside. A hooded figure nodded. A wave of fear washed over Cenaya. The hooded woman looked at Cenaya through sunken eyes. Her decaying skin and black teeth added to her terrifying appearance.

Cenaya nodded back to her, unable to utter a response.

The Creator spoke instead, "Nazra uses her influence over the Undead to further our cause of peace."

"You must learn to control your fear, Princess," Nazra cautioned. "Many, especially the Undead, use fear against their enemies."

Cenaya simply nodded again.

The Creator turned Cenaya away from Nazra. She met her father's gaze. Was that sadness in his eyes?

"Your father is also an invaluable member of our Court. I'm pleased to provide a chance for father and daughter to work together to build a better world."

Cenaya smiled weakly at her father. She felt emotionally exhausted.

"And this is the future king of Zndaria." The Creator motioned to an unusually tall, scrawny elf with rust-colored skin.

The elf bowed to her. "It's a pleasure to meet you, Princess."

Yearning masked what little fear Cenaya still felt from Nazra. She'd hardly heard her beautiful Elvish language since coming to Taycod, even from her father, except in her lessons. Curtseying, she replied in the same tongue, "Thank you for welcoming me here."

"You are very important to our cause," he continued in Elvish. "Joining us will bring peace to the land." He bowed again.

"You're all very kind," she spoke the common tongue again while looking around the group. She made sure to avoid eye contact with Nazra. "But I'm confident it will be my mother, not me, joining your Court."

"We all wish for your mother's safety and are anxious to know which beautiful queen will serve with us." The Creator placed his hand on her arm and faced his Court. "I have one more gift for the princess. I shall join you in the strategy room shortly."

Cenaya's father nodded his approval. The Court bowed to her. She curtsied in return, then followed the Creator deeper into the unknown.

Chapter Eight

THE FLETCHER

The Creator led Cenaya through another full-length mirror into a dimly lit hallway. Once again, her skin tingled from the magic. Down the hallway, they stopped at a metal door guarded by two burly imps. At the Creator's gesture, one of the imps slid a heavy bolt to the side. The other swung the door open.

The Creator ushered Cenaya inside a vast grotto. A long workbench filled with tools lined one wall. Above it hung arrows of every color, made of everything from wood, rock, and crystal to brass, silver, and gold. One even glistened like diamonds. On the opposite wall, metal shelves held countless differently shaped containers. While the smallest could fit in Cenaya's hand, the largest was as big as her torso. She couldn't read the shiny writing on each one.

A grassy field longer than the Sky Castle's courtyard filled half of the cavern. Targets varying from tall and thin to short and wide covered the field. Some spun in circles, others stood still. Some even floated in the air. She couldn't help but stare at everything.

"It seems you like my fletcher's workshop." The Creator grinned.

"It's amazing!" Cenaya gushed. "I've never seen anything like it."

"I'm glad you like my home," a timid voice spoke. "Welcome, Princess."

Cenaya turned to face a tall, thin woman stepping out from behind an iron furnace. She

♦ Scrolls of Zndaria ♦

appeared mostly human. Her rust-colored skin matched the imp guards. Glistening white horns extended out of her coarsely twisted hair. Leather goggles sat on her forehead. Wiping her hands on a thick leather apron, she bowed before the Creator.

The Creator returned the gesture with a slight bow, then turned to Cenaya. "Cenaya, this is Eva, my fletcher. She is my first, and one of my finest, creations. Her magical arrows are unlike any in all of Zndaria."

"Magical arrows?" Cenaya looked toward the wall of unique arrows.

"Yes, and you'll make several of them today to go with this." He lifted a bow from the workbench. "The second part of your birthday gift."

Cenaya took the offered weapon. She caressed the intricately carved darkwood and ran her finger along the taut string. "This is magnificent! But, sir, you've already given me so much." She gestured to her new armor. "I don't know how I can accept more."

"You are important to my Court. It's necessary that I protect you and allow you to protect yourself." He dismissed her concern. "I'll leave you with Eva to make your arrows. Your father will come for you soon."

Cenaya bowed, still astonished by the wondrous gifts she'd received. "Thank you for your generosity."

He bent forward and kissed Cenaya's hand. "Until we meet again, Princess."

Cenaya stood next to the fletcher in awkward silence. The Creator strutted out of the workshop. The thud of the bolt securing the door echoed in the grotto.

Eva turned to Cenaya and smiled. "Cenaya! I'm so happy to finally meet you." Her bubbly voice sounded nothing like the person Cenaya had just met. She rubbed her hands together. "We have lots to do! Let's get started." She wrapped her arm around Cenaya's shoulder and moved toward the shelves. "What do you want your arrows to do?"

"What do you mean, *to do*?" Cenaya looked up at the fletcher but didn't pull away from her. She appreciated the fletcher's motherly presence.

They reached the shelves, and Eva pulled down a container the size of her hand. "My arrows can do anything. We could start with one of these."

She lifted the lid and tilted the case toward Cenaya. Pudgy green beetles snapped their pincers. Their front legs slapped the side of the container.

Cenaya cringed. "How do those make an arrow?"

"An emrab beetle arrow paralyzes your attacker the same way it would if the beetle itself pinched the victim."

Cenaya sighed. "I could see how that would be helpful." Her head reeled trying to make sense of everything she'd seen today. She didn't think she could even decide about arrows.

Glancing sideways at Cenaya, the fletcher replaced the lid. "I know you've had a lot to take in." She patted Cenaya's hand. "I have the perfect thing to start with." She lifted a similar-sized container from the shelf, then moved to the workbench. She held up what looked like a clay snake. "This is your arrow's shaft." She laid it straight on the bench. "You'll only find this substance in the underworld, and only if you know where to look." She beamed. Opening the container, she pulled out a silky white worm.

Cenaya edged forward. The worm glistened. She watched closely.

The fletcher pressed the worm into the clay. "My arrows take on the property of whatever is embedded inside the shaft." She pressed two more worms into the clay and replaced the container's lid. "These silk worms wrap your attacker in a cocoon."

Cenaya grinned. She'd like to see that happen.

Laying the arrow on a metal tray, Eva fiddled with it until it was perfectly straight. She covered her eyes with her goggles and opened the furnace door.

Tears wet Cenaya's eyes. She turned away from the intense heat.

The fletcher shut the door, and the room cooled instantly. "This will just take a moment." She began humming a lively tune. Her body swayed to the rhythm.

Cenaya smiled. "You seem very happy here."

"Of course I am, dearie. Happiness is a choice and I choose to be happy in my home." She glanced at the metal door. "Though I long for the day my family and I are free in the world above."

Cenaya hadn't expected to hear that.

"One day the mist will cover Zndaria." Eva seemed lost in her thoughts. "And it'll be safe to leave the underworld."

"The mist?"

She looked at Cenaya and blinked several times, almost as if remembering she had a guest. "Oh, dear." Her eyes looked alarmed. "He told me not to mention that. It isn't important." She turned to the furnace. "Your first shaft is ready." Her bubbly voice had returned. She removed the tray. "Let's finish your arrow."

Cenaya followed her back to the workbench. *What was the mist, and why shouldn't she talk about it?* Questions began forming in Cenaya's mind. *Is there more to the Creator than I realized?*

"Choose your point." Eva pulled Cenaya from her thoughts.

Cenaya looked down. Her now-hardened shaft lay smooth and white, similar to the worms. Next to it, an array of arrowheads covered the table. She eyed the various colors, trying to guess what substances were used to make them. One looked as if made of rubies, another resembled marble. She picked up one that looked like crystals. "I like this one."

"A marvelous match!" Eva placed her goggles back on her forehead and clamped the shaft in a vise. With a swift tap of a mallet, she secured the point. She picked four white feathers from a pile of differently colored feathers and attached them to the arrow shaft equal distances apart. Using a thin blade, she chiseled a notch in the end of the shaft.

She released the vise, then handed Cenaya the arrow. "Here is your first one!"

"Thank you!" Cenaya grinned. She loved how comfortable she felt around Eva, and she loved her new arrow. She placed it in her quiver. "Can we make more?"

"Of course, dearie," the fletcher said from halfway toward the shelves. "We'll do as many as you'd like."

"It's time to go, Princess."

Cenaya jumped. She hadn't noticed her father enter the workshop. An extremely old man with wrinkly, pasty skin stood next to him. His hair consisted of a few grey patches that matched his hollow eyes. He looked like he belonged in the infirmary.

"But I was just about to practice with my arrows. Can we stay just a little longer?" Cenaya pled.

"I said it's time to go."

He wasn't mean, just firm. Cenaya knew better than to argue. She grasped the fletcher's hands in her own. "Thank you, again."

"You've been a joy." Eva kissed her cheek. "I do hope you'll come back soon."

Cenaya picked up her quiver filled with a couple dozen colorful arrows and started for the door.

"The one you requested is ready." Eva handed Cenaya's father a dull, seemingly unfinished clay arrow.

"Will it work?"

"Have my arrows ever failed you?"

"Never." Although his face remained emotionless, his eyes brightened slightly. "Thank you."

Cenaya followed her father and the old man out the door. Over her shoulder, she watched the guards secure it behind them. The Creator's world of peace held a lot of secrets and restraints. She was determined to find out why.

Chapter Nine

THE BEAST

Cenaya said little to her father or the royal family at dinner that evening. Lost in her thoughts about her visit to Shelltown and the underworld, she retired to her tower bedroom early. From her balcony, she watched the setting sun brilliantly illuminate the fluffy clouds holding the Sky Castle. The castle walls shimmered like diamonds. Different colored flames danced atop the palace's staggered turrets. She soaked up the enchantment.

Retreating back into her room, she spied her quiver resting against her dresser. She wished she'd had time to practice with the fletcher. She grinned. She could practice now. Pulling out the smooth white arrow, she returned to the balcony. Aiming at a tree near the aviary, she pulled back the bow string.

Something stole toward the gate. Cenaya looked closer and recognized her father dressed in a dark cloak on his black pegasus, Nightmare. The old man from the underworld sat behind him in the saddle. Slipping outside the castle walls, they took flight away from the setting sun.

Cenaya's shoulders stiffened. Where was he taking the old man and why as darkness fell? Target practice could wait. Tucking her quiver and bow over her shoulder, she darted from her room. An Efreeti servant met her at the aviary doors.

"Please ready Talia." She caught her breath. "I must leave immediately."

The servant returned moments later with Talia. He looked concerned. "Will you be going out by yourself, Princess?"

"No." Cenaya mounted Talia. "I'll be with my father."

She started in the same direction her father had flown. This took her over Taycod Highway and its few travelers. She'd have to fly fast to catch up with him. The purple moon, the first of the night's three moons, rose in front of her. It felt eerie being alone outside the castle, especially in the dark. Because the king forbade the princesses to leave the castle unescorted, she'd rarely been out flying once the purple moon was high in the sky.

The brisk wind signaled an approaching storm. She rubbed her bare arms. Why hadn't she grabbed a shawl? Leaning forward, she stroked Talia's mane. The heat from the animal's body warmed her slightly. They passed over a band of soldiers with a fortified wagon. Had she missed her father? Did he change direction?

A crash startled her. Talia flinched. Up ahead, a tree lay across the highway. A cloaked man—her father—removed a rope from around the tree trunk. Landing several tree lengths away, Cenaya hid among the brush. The rope dangled from the neck of Nightmare. The old man rested on a nearby stump.

Cenaya tied Talia's reins to a branch, then crept toward them.

Her father mounted Nightmare. "We'll meet at the Crossroads Inn tomorrow. Follow Taycod Highway to Old Maple Road." He nodded toward the highway. He paused and cocked his head slightly. "I hear them. I'll leave you to the task for which you were created." He flew off in the direction he'd nodded.

The old man hunkered down behind the brush.

Cenaya started for Talia. She'd follow her father to confront him. She heard creaking wagon wheels and clomping hooves and stopped. Her father was a mystery to her. Did she really expect him to be open about the old man? She might learn more if she remained hidden and watched. Taking care not to be seen or heard, she moved closer to the highway.

Several cavalry riders halted at the fallen tree. A dark-skinned knight dismounted his stallion and inspected the log. The wagon Cenaya had seen a short time earlier stopped behind them. The door swung open.

A plump young man with slicked-back hair stepped out. "Haldon!" he snapped. "Why have we stopped?"

The knight turned. "A fallen tree is blocking the road. We'll clear our path and be on our way."

"No! We will make camp here." The young man stamped his foot. "You said we'd push on until we reached the inn for dinner, but we've stopped again. I'm starving."

Haldon approached the wagon. "Young Lord Brade, we're all hungry, but our rest will be sounder if we make it to the inn tonight."

The old man shifted in his hiding place.

"Your duty is to see to my safety and comfort until I reach the Halls of Magic. I'll rest just fine on my bed in the wagon. If we don't eat soon, I'll tell my father that you starved me and kept the rations for yourself."

Haldon walked back to the tree. Several cavalry riders joined him. He looked back at the wagon, his face tight. He motioned to the riders. "You three set up camp. The others and I will clear the road. We'll set out again at first light."

"Yes, sir." The cavalry riders' stern faces didn't hide their frustration with the orders.

Smirking, the young man stepped back into the wagon and slammed the door behind him.

The soldiers made camp in a clearing across the road from Cenaya. The old man settled in with his back against a tree.

What was his task? Cenaya watched him carefully. It looked like he'd fallen asleep. Was the escort party in danger? Could an unarmed old man hurt them? If not, why had her father caused them to stop?

Cenaya hunched back against the tree. Her stomach grumbled, and she shivered. The camp's dinner smelled wonderful. Their fire looked inviting. The purple moon drooped in the sky. She pulled some fallen branches over her. They warmed her just enough. She'd stay until the middle of the night when the orange moon peaked. If she didn't understand the old man's purpose by then, she'd have to return home.

Most of the soldiers retired to their tents. The pompous young man strutted to the war wagon. Haldon and another knight stayed by the fire, and stillness settled over the camp. The old man remained asleep against the tree.

The orange moon peaked over the horizon. She'd only wait a little longer.

Voices drifted from the campsite. Cenaya stirred. She'd fallen asleep.

Stretching, Haldon stood from the fire. "In a few days, young Lord Brade will be at the Halls, and we will rest well. Good night, men."

Two soldiers took their posts as guards. The

red moon rose through the trees. Cenaya had slept until early in the morning. She glanced at the old man. He hadn't changed position. She sighed and arched her back. She'd be returning to the castle without any answers.

Movement caught her eye. The old man no longer slept. He stole deeper into the forest. Cenaya darted after him, leaving Talia secured to the tree. She rushed ahead. The anticipation of discovery filled her with energy.

The old man stopped in a smaller clearing. Moonlight directly overhead bathed him. His hunched body quaked. His shredded clothing fell to the ground. Massive paws with razor-sharp claws replaced his hands. His face became a gruesome sight with a monstrous snout and glowing eyes. He was no longer the withered old man. Now covered in fur, he'd transformed into a towering beast.

Dread washed over Cenaya.

The beast let out a terrifying roar and lumbered toward the camp.

♦ Scrolls of Zndaria ♦

Cenaya stood paralyzed with fear. The sound of trees crashing to the ground rocked the night. Two horses galloping toward her broke her trance. She dove out of the way. Picking herself up, she rushed to the camp, toward the horrific sounds of clashing metal, screaming soldiers, and the beast's deafening roars. She had to help!

Cenaya readied a dark-blue arrow in her bow. Surely an ice blast would stop him. Reaching the campsite, she skidded to a stop. Two soldiers lay in front of her, a blood-stained sword and battered axe by their sides. Their helmets had been knocked to the ground, their skulls crushed. Her heart pounded. The war wagon lay on its side, marred by long claw marks. Its door dangled on one hinge.

Cenaya hurried around the wagon. The beast slashed the man they'd called Haldon across the back, throwing him into the nearby brush. Cenaya gasped. Haldon didn't move. The beast staggered toward her. She aimed her bow at him. Blood oozed from countless slashes in his flesh, evidence of his struggles with the soldiers. His mighty shoulders slumped. He didn't roar, growl, or even snarl at her.

Cenaya lowered her bow. In his dimly glowing, hollow eyes, she didn't see a terrifying beast. She saw a weak old man riddled with fatal wounds. He couldn't hurt anyone else. Lightning lit up the night sky. The beast cowered away under the start of a cold drizzle.

Cenaya looked around the camp. Memories of the guards who died protecting their fortress the night of the Swamp Witch's attack flooded her mind. She replaced her arrow in her quiver and shouldered her bow. How could she save these men? She ran to Haldon. "Sir! Can you hear me?"

"Yes," he strained to speak. "But I can't free myself."

Cenaya gripped his ankles and pulled as hard as she could. The brush trembled under him, but he didn't budge.

"I can't move." He coughed. "Please—" he gasped for breath. "Please get help."

Cenaya looked around. No one else showed signs of life. If they had survived, she couldn't help them by herself. She knew it would take her the rest of the night to get to the castle and back. Her father had mentioned an inn. Perhaps someone there could help.

"I'll return as soon as I'm able." She darted toward Talia.

She thought the man grunted a thank you, but she didn't take time to reply. She had to hurry. She might be his only chance to live.

Chapter Ten

THE CROSSROADS INN

Gripping Talia's reins tightly, Cenaya flew above Taycod Highway. The wind howled around them. The rain pelted her face. Was the inn close? Should she have returned to the castle?

She eyed a three-story building up ahead. Sighing in relief, she landed near the decrepit front steps. Its decaying walls sagged. Warped extra-wide double doors hung crookedly on their rusty iron hinges. Broken shutters banged loudly.

Tying Talia to the railing, she rushed inside. A tavern filled the entire main floor, but only two patrons remained.

A plump satyr sat at the back table with a large pitcher of brown liquid. "Welcome to the Crossroads Inn." His words almost strung together. He held out his mug. "Want some bubbler ta warm ya up?"

At a different table, a man hooded in a dark cloak with his head hung low turned around. He looked surprised to see her.

"Father!" Cenaya rushed to him. "Those men are hurt! We must help them!"

He took a long drink from his bubbler and looked straight ahead. "It is as it must be, Princess."

Cenaya couldn't believe what she heard. "Did you know this would happen?" She didn't mean to yell but couldn't contain her outrage. "Did you intend for those men to die?"

He stood with such swiftness that she recoiled from him. He gripped her arm. "I will speak with

♦ The Alamist Queen ♦

you outside."

He pulled her behind him. His fingers dug into her arm. He threw the doors open, and the cold rain blew into their faces. He dropped his arm to his side. Cenaya stepped away from him. She'd never seen him like this, and it frightened her.

"My Princess," he spoke gently and reached for her. She took another step backward. His head drooped. "Princess." He faced her again with sagging shoulders and barely spoke over the wind. "I follow the Creator's orders without question. I do not control or determine the outcome."

Cenaya stared at him. Strands of rain-soaked hair escaped the tie behind his head and stuck to his face. The wind fluttered the arrows in their quivers. The cold rain hitting her face only increased her anger.

"That's it!" she screamed. "You were just following orders?" She shivered both from anger and the cold. "Well, I don't take orders from the Creator. I'm going to save those men! Are you going to help me, or do I have to find someone else?" She stomped down the steps to untie Talia.

Her father took the reins out of her hands. "No, Princess." He stood firmly in front of her. "You will not find anyone else at this time of night, and you've already been in this weather too long. You don't look well."

"I'm just fine!" She lunged for the reins.

He easily moved them out of her reach.

She shivered again, more deeply. She didn't want to admit the truth. Tears stung her eyes worse than the rain. "But what about those men?" She choked on tears and rain. "How can I just let them die?"

He placed his arm around her shoulders. "I wish that this was your decision to make." He sounded sincere.

His arms warmed her. She dropped her head, unable to fight anymore.

Pressing a key into her hand, he moved her toward the steps. "Go in and get some rest. I'll care for Talia." He squeezed her a little bit closer.

"I'm sorry, My Princess."

Entering the tavern, Cenaya climbed the stairs, numb to everything around her. The groan of each step echoed how she felt inside. On the top floor, she swung the room door open. A dank odor greeted her. The dim light from the hallway torch revealed a warped wooden floor coated in dust, two simple hay beds, and a rusty candlestick near a small wash basin. She didn't want to see more.

She felt defeated and now that she accepted it, she felt faint. Closing the door behind her, she removed her breastplate and lay on the bed. Tucking the quilt around her wet, shivering body, she wept. In one day, her life had turned upside down. She'd seen the poverty in Shelltown, met the Creator and his Court, and learned her father was a murderer. She struggled to fall asleep with so many thoughts rattling her mind.

The next morning, she awoke under a second quilt. Her father must've placed it on her, but when? She glanced around the empty room.

Walking to the window, she shivered only slightly this time. Her clothes were nearly dry.

Dense clouds hid the sun. A brisk wind scattered thick maple leaves from the surrounding forest across the yard. The barren trees trembled in the cold drizzle. Withered plants looked like mere shadows of their former selves. Her stomach growled. *How long did I sleep? Is it time for breakfast or lunch?*

She looked in the mirror. Dark lines streaked her face. Emptying a pitcher into the basin, she cringed. Yesterday, she woke up in her lavish castle bedroom. Today, she scooped murky water in her hands and splashed her face. Everything had changed.

A light knock sounded on the door, and her father entered. He wore his breastplate instead of his dark cloak. Cenaya turned away. The sight of him made her want to cry.

"I've paid for your meal. I'll prepare the animals and give you time to eat. We'll leave when you're done, with or without the old man."

Cenaya thought she heard remorse in his voice, but she didn't ask. She pulled on her breastplate and followed him downstairs. He didn't question her silence. She pictured the injured beast. If she could speak to her father, she'd tell him the old man wouldn't be joining them.

In the tavern, a group of laughing and singing patrons seemed to enjoy their bubbler. The plump satyr from the night before lay on his table in a drunken stupor. His head hung off the edge. Drool dripped from his gaping mouth into a pool of slobber on the floor.

The burly bar maiden handed Cenaya a steaming bowl and a cup of juice. "Red pea gumbo and hollyapple juice." She didn't smile and almost seemed cross. "Sit wherever you'd like."

"Thank you." Cenaya took the meal and settled into a table near the door. She'd never seen gumbo before. Picking through the combination of vegetables and meats, she scooped out a bite of vegetables. It tasted wonderful and warmed her insides.

A grinning halfling bounced up to Cenaya. Her bright-pink pointed hat matched her ankle-length dress and partially covered her curly hair. "Hello! My friends and I are from the Halls of Magic." She waved to three male halfings sitting at a different table. Their eyes just peeked out of snug green caps. "Are you going there today?"

"No." Cenaya didn't feel like talking.

"That's too bad!" The halfling sounded bubbly, but her eyes looked cold. "We really like to greet new visitors." She left Cenaya and rejoined her companions.

Cenaya ate another bite. A short elf entered the tavern. His eyes shone with confidence. He strutted to the bar, leading the way for a lanky young man in crisp wool pants, a cotton shirt, and tan jerkin. The young man's brown eyes darted around. Cenaya dug through her gumbo for a meatless bite. She appreciated its warmth sliding down her throat. Glancing up, she met the young man's eyes.

"May I help you?" Cenaya spoke in the common tongue.

"Ah . . . n-n-no," the young man stammered. Blushing, he tried to smile, but it looked painful. He hurried away.

Cenaya couldn't help but chuckle inside. She slurped another bite and took a long drink, emptying her mug. She approached the bar. "May I have more juice, please?"

The bar maiden took the cup without a word. Cenaya looked around the tavern. The female halfling approached the short elf and his lanky friend along the back wall. Something didn't feel right. She focused her elf hearing on their conversation.

"Hello! I'm Mysty." The halfling touched the elf's shoulder. "My friends and I are in town picking up supplies for the Halls of Magic. I haven't seen you around here before."

"What a coincidence." The short elf grinned. "We're also on our way to the Halls of Magic. I'm

Blinkly, and this is Nate. He's a wizard in training."

"N-n-no, I'm not." A look of panic crossed the young man's face. "He just likes to make up stories."

The bar maiden cleared her throat. "Your juice, Your Highness."

If she hadn't been so intent on figuring out the motives of the strange halfling, Cenaya would've been annoyed by the bite in the bar maiden's voice. "Thank you." She looked toward the bar maiden just long enough to take the mug.

The halfling skipped over to her own table. She didn't say anything, just nodded toward the two young men. The male halflings rose immediately. She skipped back. The males followed her, but didn't share her lightheartedness.

The young men stood when the halflings reached their table.

The female didn't wait for them to say anything. "My full name is Mystria. This is Twin

Blade, Iron Fist, and Double Claw."

Those aren't halfling names. Cenaya set her cup on the bar.

The elf echoed her thoughts, "How'd you get names like those?"

"Like this." The female removed her hat. It vanished. She grew from a halfling to a tall, pale lady with long blood-red hair. The sleeves of her dress flared at her wrist. The hem brushed her knees.

Cenaya gasped.

One of the male halflings removed his cap. It also vanished. He immediately transformed into a muscular dwarf with a single long black tuft of hair protruding from the back of his head. He wore chain mail armor. A tattoo of a ten-legged black spider with blood dripping from its fangs covered his thick neck. He pulled two razor-sharp hatchets from the sheaths at his waist.

In the same instant, the other two halflings removed their caps. One grew into a bulky human about the height of the young man and stared into his eyes. He had a full beard. His curly black hair hung down to the shoulders of his spiked iron breastplate. He held a spiked club in his right hand. A solid iron fist replaced his left hand.

Cenaya heard the young man's gasp from across the room.

The other halfling grew until he stood several boot-lengths taller than his companions. His bulky frame resembled a troll with hairy ears and feet. In place of his hands, two large metal claws kept snapping together.

The boys stepped back. The troll clutched the young man around the neck with his right claw. He lifted him high into the air and slammed him up against the wall. Something clattered to the floor.

The bar patrons rushed to the front doors. Cenaya fought through them to her bow at her table.

"I'll have none of that in my tavern!" the bar maiden bellowed. "Git outta here now!"

"Batista!" Mystria sounded entertained.

Grabbing her bow, Cenaya swung her quiver over her shoulder. She turned around just in time to see the bar maiden stumble backward, away from a swarm of bats flying toward her. A crossbow flew from her hands. Striking her head against the wall, she slumped to the floor. The bats collided with the bar and evaporated. Mystria turned and faced the boy held against the wall.

Cenaya pulled a white arrow from her quiver.

"You don't look like a wizard." Mystria picked a wand up off the floor and rolled it in her fingers. "But we're paid just to stop you from reaching the Halls." Mysteria threw the wand. "Kill them!"

Cenaya aimed at Mystria. "Release them!"

Mystria faced her and smirked, "Your arrow is no match for me!"

"Catch it, then!" Cenaya released the white arrow. *This better work!*

Just before it struck Mystria's forehead, she caught it in her right hand and jeered.

Cenaya held her breath.

The arrow stretched into a long silky thread. It swiftly enveloped Mystria's body, encasing her in a silky cocoon. The cocoon fell to the ground with a thud.

Yes! It worked even better than Cenaya had expected. The bulky human pointed his fist at her. She pulled a dark-blue arrow from her quiver. The fist detached from his arm. She aimed the arrow. The fist struck her in the chest.

Pain seared through her body. She fell backward, slamming her head against the table. Darkness wrapped around her.

Chapter Eleven

RECOVERY

"Is she healing?"

Cenaya lay still, keeping her eyes shut. The Creator stood over her. Her head ached. She remembered trying to help the boys at the inn, but nothing after that. Where was she now?

"Yes." Her father's voice calmed her, slightly. "But the blow to her head may cause her to sleep for several more days. Gratefully, your armor protected her from more severe injuries."

♦ Scrolls of Zndaria ♦

"As it is intended to do. But why was she at the inn?" The Creator sounded disturbed. "Who allowed her to leave unescorted?"

Cenaya bit the inside of her lip.

"She told the servant she would be with me."

The Creator chuckled. "Curious, just like you. Perhaps her curiosity will lead her just as easily down the same road. She definitely knows how to find trouble."

Cenaya cringed.

"She was just trying to help."

"You stopped my mercenaries!" the Creator said.

Cenaya's body tensed. Pain shot through her chest. She had to ignore it.

"Because of your interference, he got away from them!"

"I would've protected my daughter even if she wasn't the next Alamist Queen."

The Creator laughed out loud.

Cenaya's stomach churned.

"It doesn't matter." She could hear the sneer

♦ The Alamist Queen ♦

in his voice. "The beast completed his task and killed him that night."

The Beast? Bloody scenes from the campsite flashed through her mind. *But the beast was dead!* Dread washed over her again. She shivered, but sweat dripped down her cheek. She feared the Creator would notice she'd awoken.

"Now that the boy is dead, it's just a matter of time until Zndaria is fully under my control." The Creator paused. "When your daughter becomes the Alamist Queen, we'll hasten our attacks and finally bring this war to an end."

His last sentence chilled her. How could she ever serve this vile man?

Cenaya heard one set of footsteps start away from her.

"We should let her rest." Her father's voice floated from further away.

Someone leaned closer to her. "Sleep well, my queen." The Creator's voice caused a chill to run down her spine. "Your recovery is vital to my strategy."

Another set of footsteps walked away from her. The door closed behind them, and her room fell silent.

Cenaya shuddered. *How could the beast still be alive?* She wanted to sob but worried they'd return. *I saw his wounds! He shouldn't have survived!* Her thoughts tumbled over everything she'd overheard. *Father spoke as if the old man's task was to stop the escort party. Who else did he kill? How would a boy have stopped the Creator?* She'd followed her father to find answers, not to end up with more questions.

She needed to figure out what was going on. Deciding they wouldn't return, she opened her eyes and sat up. The royal recovery room spun around her. She felt sick to her stomach. Wiping her sweaty hands on her bed sheets, she sat back against her pillow and closed her eyes. Sliding down into the sheets, she pulled the covers over her head. She'd have to think about it more when her head stopped throbbing.

♦ The Alamist Queen ♦

Cenaya woke to sunlight coming through the window beside her feather bed. She blinked several times before noticing Kathlyn sitting beside her.

Kathlyn put down the book she'd been reading and stroked Cenaya's hair. "How are you feeling today?"

Cenaya sat up slowly, pressing her hand against her chest. "Like I was knocked over by a boulder. How long have I been asleep?"

"A couple of days. I've sat with you each day. I wanted to be here when you woke up." Rising, she filled a plate from a nearby table and placed it on Cenaya's lap. She held a cup of juice out to her. "Can you eat or drink any of this?"

Cenaya took the cup and drained it. It coated her parched throat. "Thank you." She handed the cup back. "Could I get some more?"

Kathlyn smiled and turned to refill the juice.

Cenaya's stomach released a deep growl. She took a bite of bread and finished the entire roll before Kathlyn returned with her juice. She drank three more cups by the time she'd cleared her plate.

Settling back into her chair, Kathlyn lifted her book from the stand. "Would you like me to read to you?"

Cenaya nestled back into her pillow. "Why are you doing all this?" she sighed. "You're here taking care of me. You took me to Shelltown. Why? I've practically ignored you for the last few years."

Kathlyn touched Cenaya's arm. "You've been special to me from the day you arrived. I saw you being influenced by my father and sisters and was waiting for the right time to help you see who you were meant to be. That's why I took you to Shelltown." She lifted the book again. "I'm helping you because I care about you. Now let yourself rest."

Cenaya closed her eyes and listened to Kathlyn read. At some point during the story about a far-off world with mechanical dragons, metal horses, and steel buildings that soared thousands of boot-lengths into the sky, she drifted off to sleep.

For the next few days, Kathlyn greeted Cenaya each morning. She served her meals, brought her clean clothes, and kept her spirits up. She spent more time with Cenaya than the royal physician did.

A week after she first awoke, Cenaya opened her eyes to someone different. Prince Davien sat in the chair beside her, looking as handsome as always.

"Good morning, beautiful." He smiled gently. "How are you feeling?"

Cenaya's heart leapt, thrilled to see him and yet, panicking at the same time. She ran her fingers through her hair.

He grinned at her.

She sighed. "I get a little better every day."

"I'm glad." He brushed her hair out of her eyes. "I've been very worried about you. Thank goodness your father was there to save you."

"Yes," Cenaya cringed. "I'm grateful he helped

me." She hated that she'd needed to be saved and despised the memory of why she'd been there.

"I've brought you a gift." He slipped a sapphire and gold bracelet onto her wrist. "I want you to know I'm always thinking of you."

Cenaya ran her fingers over the glistening gems. "Thank you! It's beautiful!"

"Just like you." He sat back, smiling proudly. "I've also been wanting to tell you that Father's decided it's time I assist in running the kingdom. I've been appointed a captain in his army."

Cenaya settled back against her pillow. She loved watching him talk. His chiseled features caused flutters in her stomach.

"I now command the courtyard guards. It's the first of many important positions I'll hold." Enthusiasm radiated from him. He detailed his numerous duties, then rose from his chair. "I'm afraid I must leave." He kissed her hand that now wore his bracelet. "May I take you to dinner when you're fully recovered?"

"I'd love that," Cenaya grinned.

"Then I'll leave you to rest." He bowed and met her grin. "Until then."

Watching him leave, Cenaya sighed. She wished he didn't have to go. Kathlyn joined her later. Cenaya still felt elated about the prince's visit, but not knowing how Kathlyn would respond, she didn't say anything about it.

Cenaya now felt well enough to get out of bed for a moment, if she moved slowly. Cenaya and Kathlyn moved together to fill their plates for lunch. She reached in front of Kathlyn for the fruit. Kathlyn's eyes fell on her wrist and her new bracelet.

Cenaya grinned sheepishly. "It's beautiful, isn't it? Prince Davien gave it to me this morning."

"Yes, it is." Kathlyn smiled but looked sad. She placed some fruit on her own plate. "Please be guarded, Cenaya. Not everyone in the castle is how they seem."

Cenaya didn't know how to respond. She fought off her old thoughts of Kathlyn's constant negativity. She finished filling her plate and returned to her bed. They ate in silence for some time. When they spoke again, they said nothing about Prince Davien or the bracelet.

Several days later, as Kathlyn quietly read to Cenaya, her sisters burst into the room.

Victoria reached her bed first. "What are you doing in here?" She frowned at Kathlyn. "You need to leave so we can spend time with Cenaya."

Kathlyn stood slowly. "I'm glad you decided to visit her. Have you seen her since the day you went to the Lamp?" She patted Cenaya's hand. "I'll come back later."

The three princesses stood with their arms crossed, glaring at Kathlyn.

Cenaya placed her hand over Kathlyn's. "Thank you."

Before Kathlyn had closed the door, Victoria sat on the side of Cenaya's bed. The bounce hurt Cenaya's chest. "Can you believe she has the nerve to come see you after she kidnapped you? She should be ashamed of herself!"

"She's so inconsiderate to others!" Abigail

jostled the other side.

Cenaya gritted her teeth.

Abigail continued without taking a breath. "After she took you, the guards escorted us home and then returned to the Lamp to join in the search. Our entire outing was ruined!"

Elizabeth filled a plate from the food table. "I've never been so angry with Kathlyn as I was that day. Father says it'll be a long time until we get to go back to the Lamp."

"She should be banished from our kingdom," Victoria smirked. "She doesn't want to be here anyway."

"Do you three know about Shelltown?" Cenaya looked to each of them.

"Everyone knows about that awful place," Victoria snapped.

Elizabeth waved a slice of bread in the air. "Father says it's full of danger and disease. I don't know why the Efreet choose to live there!"

"They don't have a choice." Cenaya exhaled her frustration. "Your father makes sure of that!"

♦ Scrolls of Zndaria ♦

Abigail stroked Cenaya's hair. Cenaya felt like a baby animal. "You poor dear. Kathlyn's been filling your head with her stories."

Cenaya jerked her head away from Abigail's hand. It made her dizzy, but her anger steadied her. "They aren't stories! The way they're treated isn't fair!"

Elizabeth pressed her lips together. "Whatever Kathlyn is telling you isn't true. It's just a way for her to make us feel guilty for living happy lives. Remember, she wants everyone to be as miserable as she is."

"No," Cenaya insisted. "She wants things to be fair for everyone."

Shaking her head, Victoria rose from the bed. "You'd better get some more rest, Cenaya." She started toward the door and motioned for her sisters to follow her. "We'll visit you again when you're thinking straight."

Cenaya could only stare as they closed the door behind them. Had that really just happened? Worse, is that how she used to act? No wonder

Kathlyn worried about her.

Kathlyn returned later that day. Cenaya didn't mention what her sisters had said. She didn't agree with them. Kathlyn continued coming each day. Her sisters didn't visit again. Cenaya appreciated both.

Several weeks later, the physician released Cenaya from the recovery room with strict instructions to obey the castle rules. She didn't hesitate to agree, knowing she didn't have a choice. She also knew her days of blindly following the king's, her father's, or anyone else's orders had passed.

Chapter Twelve

ESCAPE

Cenaya brushed Talia's mane. Since her release from the recovery ward a couple of weeks ago, she'd flown her as much as possible. Just like tonight, she often flew around the courtyard and castle turrets until well after sunset when most of the castle slept. She longed to fly over Wishington and the surrounding forest but had only once been permitted an escort outside the castle walls. The guards kept an extra close watch over her. She almost felt like a prisoner.

"I thought I'd find you here."

Recognizing the voice, Cenaya smiled at her visitor. She'd spent a lot of time with Kathlyn as well. The other princesses often expressed their disapproval, but Cenaya ignored them.

Kathlyn propped a knapsack against the stall door next to Cenaya's bow and arrows. She placed a bucket of oats in front of Talia. Looking around, she stepped closer to Cenaya. "The servants are escaping tonight," she whispered.

Cenaya nearly dropped the brush. "What do you mean," she lowered her voice, "escaping?"

"They have no other choice. The Efreet will never be free in Taycod." Kathlyn touched Cenaya's shoulder. "I want you to come with us."

Cenaya sank against the stall. Was she hearing all this correctly? "Why did you say *us*? Are you going, too?"

Kathlyn nodded. "I know this is sudden, but it finally came together today." She handed Cenaya the knapsack. "I grabbed a few things for you. Please come with us now. You'll have a chance to decide if you want to join us after we meet up with the others."

Sighing, Cenaya shouldered the bag and her quiver. She wanted more information before she'd agree to go anywhere. "What's the plan?"

Kathlyn lifted the window to the courtyard in Talia's stall and pulled Cenaya closer. A mule dragon flew through the castle gates, barely fitting. A giant steel crate secured by thick chains swayed beneath it. Although as big as the Lord Dragon Cenaya had encountered weeks earlier, the docile mule dragon didn't intimidate her. Instead of molten scales and smoldering wings, it had a hairy body and leathery wings. With a mule head and stringy tail, it looked friendly.

"Haze purchased the dragon and crate from one of the kingdom's suppliers. We're replacing a normal delivery so we'll leave the castle fully stocked with provisions. Once the crate is emptied, the Efreet will fill it, and we'll leave unnoticed. All the servants are gathering. Follow me."

Kathlyn led Cenaya past Nightmare and a few other pegasi used to transport non-flying guests to and from the Sky Castle. They stopped in the shadows of the stalls directly across from the supply room. Normally it only contained barrels, some full of food and supplies, others empty. Tonight, every Efreet from the castle had crammed into the space. Cenaya hadn't realized so many served there.

The driver lowered the crate directly outside the aviary doors with only a slight bang. It covered almost the entire opening. Several Efreet rushed through the little space remaining and started unhooking the chains from the dragon. Everyone else worked to empty the provisions.

A Djinni guard approached them from the castle. "Good evening, princesses."

Cenaya tensed. Would he see the gathered Efreet? Would he report them?

The guard gripped Kathlyn's hands. "Thank

♦ Scrolls of Zndaria ♦

you for everything you're doing to help the Efreet and for letting me come with you."

Kathlyn smiled. "Thank you!"

He bowed, then helped empty the crate.

Cenaya still couldn't believe any of this was happening. She peered into the courtyard. Now unattached, the dragon landed and flopped onto its belly. Its driver slid off it. A scarf hid his face, and a long cloak shrouded his body. He spoke to one of the guards before starting toward the aviary.

Grinning, Kathlyn took a step out of the shadows.

Once inside, the driver removed his scarf. Rushing to Kathlyn, he wrapped his arms around her waist and kissed her. "This is going to work!" Haze beamed. "Everyone else is ready. They're waiting for us." Still holding Kathlyn around the waist, he turned to Cenaya. "I'm glad to see you here."

They looked so happy together. Would Cenaya be that happy with Prince Davien?

The Efreet began settling into the crate.

Kathlyn pulled away. "It's almost time."

Haze crossed to Talia's stall.

Kathlyn took Cenaya's hands. "Please come with us now. Mayah wants to see you again."

Haze returned with Talia fully saddled and Cenaya's bow attached. He held the reins out to her.

"That's why I recognized you!" Cenaya took Talia's reins from Haze just as she'd done at her birthday party. "You brought her into the ballroom!"

"Yes," Haze grinned. "And I've trained her well. She has many magical abilities and will know what is needed tonight. Are you coming?"

Cenaya couldn't bear the thought of not saying goodbye to Mayah. "Yes, of course!"

"Thank you!" Kathlyn wrapped Cenaya in an embrace. "There's a shawl in your knapsack."

Haze took Kathlyn's hand, and they started toward the exit. "Stand ready beside the crate and fly away from the guards. They should be too distracted to see you leave with us."

Haze exited with several Efreet. Cenaya wrapped the shawl around her shoulders and mounted Talia. Kathlyn entered the crate. Haze scurried up onto the dragon's back and guided it into the air. The Efreet reattached the chains. Two Djinn guards watching the small openings between the crate and the supply room whispered between themselves. Cenaya moved behind the crate. She heard the shuffling of footsteps.

"Halt!" the guards barked from outside. The footsteps stopped. "We need to inspect the crate," one voice said. "Something is going on. We've seen far too much movement in there."

Cenaya locked eyes with Kathlyn. This would ruin everything. Haze couldn't help. With the chains attached, he had to keep the dragon hovering. The footsteps started again.

Kathlyn started out of the crate. Cenaya held her palm up to stop her. She pulled an arrow made with the sleeping dust of a caterpillar from her quiver and stepped to the corner. The guards followed the four Efreet in from the courtyard. Remaining out of their view, Cenaya released her arrow. It struck at the feet of the guards. Light-blue smoke rose around them. Both the Efreet and the guards fell to the ground in a deep sleep.

"I need several strong Efreet and the Djinni guard!" Cenaya insisted. They rushed to the sleeping victims. "You four get your friends into the crate." She instructed the Efreet, then turned to the Djinni guard. "Tell Haze to give us just a moment and then get us out of here."

He rushed out, flying to where Haze watched helplessly from above. Haze nodded.

The guard returned to the crate. Once he made it inside, the Efreet pulled massive ropes to close it. Cenaya watched for it to move. She didn't like waiting. They needed to leave. Finally, it lifted from the ground.

Cenaya nudged Talia upward, matching the crate's rise. She followed behind it until they neared the castle wall. The dragon rose, and she moved above it, shielding herself from the view of

♦ Scrolls of Zndaria ♦

the turret guards. She glanced behind her continually, waiting for a guard to stop them. No one seemed to notice her or anything suspicious.

They flew toward the southern coast. Cenaya relaxed the more their distance from the castle grew. She welcomed her stolen freedom even though she'd be in trouble when she returned. Haze veered to his left. She did the same. He shed his cloak and scarf, revealing a slick suit covering his entire body down to his wrists and feet. A few moments later, they flew over Shelltown. Haze said the others waited for them, but where? The town appeared abandoned. Cenaya saw no movement, not even a glimmer of light.

Haze didn't land but continued to the shore. He pointed downward. Tucking his body close to the mule dragon, he led it into a dive and disappeared into the ocean.

Talia pulled on the reins to follow. Cenaya hovered for a moment, then leaned into a dive. She had to trust Haze and Talia. Talia's horn began glowing a brilliant blue. A bubble of the same color grew from the tip of the horn until it surrounded them. Cenaya stared in amazement as Talia dove underwater. The bubble protected them, keeping her completely dry and able to breathe. Talia's shining horn illuminated the sea around them.

The mule dragon paddled through the water with its enormous paws. The crate dragged behind it. Lying flat on the dragon, Haze grinned at Cenaya. His wet hair pressed against his head. He didn't have a shield around him but didn't struggle for breath. He waved for her to follow.

Talia flapped her wings. The bubble glided through the ocean, brushing along seaweed covering the ocean floor. Cenaya watched in awe. A school of fish swam beside them. Several dolphins darted between Talia and the mule dragon. A swarm of jelly fish bounced off the bubble. It all felt like a dream. They rounded an underwater cliff covered with spiny, pink flowers.

Thrusting forward, the mule dragon blasted through a wall of kelp. Talia did the same. Light pierced the water above them. The mule dragon disappeared into it. Talia followed without Cenaya's encouragement. She gripped the reins. They shot out of the sea. Water sprayed away from the bubble.

Talia hovered within a gigantic cavern. Glowing crystals covered the cavern's ceiling. Cenaya shielded her eyes. The brightness matched the sunniest day. Talia's horn dimmed, and their shield disappeared.

Haze guided the mule dragon to deposit the crate onto a sandy beach. Countless pearl crabs scurried about. Men rushed to remove the chains and open the crate. Hundreds more Efreet surrounded numerous glimmering whales strewn along the beach. Cenaya first wondered if the whales were dead, then wondered if they were real. Something about them looked odd. Haze landed in front of them. The Efreet poured out of the crate completely dry. Cenaya landed beside Haze. The pearl crabs seemed unfazed by her or the Efreet.

Haze slid off the dragon. Shaking his head, he sprinkled Cenaya with water droplets. He removed a blue orb from his mouth and placed it in a small pocket in his suit. "You did great, girl!" He stroked Talia's mane, then turned to Cenaya. "I told you she'd know what to do."

"She was amazing!" Cenaya dismounted. "What other secrets does she have?"

"I'll show you once we've reached our refuge," Haze smiled.

Cenaya bit her lip. She'd have to decide soon.

Kathlyn rushed to throw her arms around Haze. "This is it!" She beamed. "We can finally be free!"

The Djinni guard from the aviary ran across the beach and embraced a young Efreeti woman near the whales.

"Princess! Princess!" a young voice called to Cenaya halfway across the beach.

Turning to the voice, Cenaya spied Mayah riding on the back of a giant pearl crab. At least, it sounded like Mayah. It didn't look like her.

Both red eyes sparkled. Her full lips grinned. Her perfect skin glowed.

"Look at me, Princess." The little girl raised her arms toward Cenaya. "Because of you, now I really am beautiful!"

Cenaya lifted her from the crab and squeezed her tightly. "You were always beautiful!" Cenaya kissed her once-deformed cheek. "Is the pain gone?"

"All of it!" Mayah's smile filled her face. Her straight teeth gleamed. "I made something for you." She wriggled out of Cenaya's arms, then pulled a leather band dotted with bits of pearl crab shell from her pocket. "Thank you for being my best friend!" She slipped it onto Cenaya's wrist over the bracelet from Prince Davien.

Cenaya couldn't speak. She twisted the gift around her wrist. Next to the dazzling bracelet, it looked simple and plain, but it meant just as much to Cenaya. She cleared her throat. "Thank you!" She gave Mayah another hug.

Grabbing Cenaya's hand, Mayah pulled her

across the sand. "Let me show you how we're getting out of here."

Kathlyn followed behind them. Cenaya could see her wide smile with the slightest turn of her head.

Mayah bounced with excitement. "We made the whales the same way we made our homes."

Stretching along the beach, the massive vessels loomed in front of them. They were twice as tall as Cenaya. She ran her hand across the fused pearl shells. "Where did you get so many shells?"

"From the beach," Mayah stated simply. "Come see inside!"

Kathlyn spoke behind them, "Pearl crabs shed their shells every summer as they grow. This is their home, so there are always plenty to collect."

Mayah pulled Cenaya through a wide opening on the side. Cenaya didn't have to duck. She guessed several hundred Efreet could easily fill the inside. Benches with attached straps of rope surrounded a small contraption resembling the

♦ Scrolls of Zndaria ♦

steamer at the Lamp.

Mayah tugged Cenaya's hand. "Come look at its sparkling eyes!"

Passing secured boxes marked "Supplies," Cenaya marveled at the front of the vessel. Two enormous crystals fused into the shells directly above an attached metal wheel acted as windows to the outside.

"Brilliant, isn't it?" Kathlyn had joined them. "The crystals allow us to see out and light the way."

"It's unbelievable! Who came up with all this?"

Kathlyn grinned. "Haze, of course."

"Everyone to their assigned vessel!" Haze's voice carried from outside.

Mayah jumped up and down, pulling on Cenaya's arm and grinning. "This is our whale so we're all ready to go!"

Tears sprang up in Cenaya's eyes. The king kept her cooped up in the castle, but she still cared deeply for Prince Davien. Her father's actions crushed her, but there was more she

♦ The Alamist Queen ♦

needed to understand. As badly as she wanted to leave with them, she felt she needed to stay. Crouching down, she stroked Mayah's perfect face. "I wish I could go with you." From the corner of her eye, Cenaya saw Kathlyn's face droop.

Mayah looked confused. "But you can, there's plenty of room."

Cenaya swallowed to steady her voice. "Right now, I need to be in Wishington." She pulled Mayah close to her and held her tightly. She kissed Mayah's cheek.

Tears flowed down Mayah's face. "Will I ever see you again?"

"I hope so." Cenaya wiped the tears from Mayah's face and then her own.

Cenaya stood and faced Kathlyn. Tears wet their cheeks. They held each other. Words couldn't express Cenaya's pain and conflict. She hoped her choice to stay was the right one.

Chapter Thirteen

PRINCE DAVIEN

"Cenaya! Cenaya wake up!"

Cenaya forced her eyes open. A figure loomed over her in the darkness. "What's wrong, Abigail?"

Abigail yanked open the curtains. Sunlight spilled in.

Cenaya squinted and covered her eyes with her hand.

"They're gone! The servants are all gone!" The

panic in Abigail's voice heightened. "Come on!"

Cenaya wrapped her robe around her shoulders, covering her clothes from the day before. She'd returned home so late she didn't bother changing before falling asleep. She hurried after Abigail. Just inside the dining hall, Cenaya stopped and stared.

Light pouring through the stained-glass windows cast a rainbow of color over the bare dining room table. Victoria and Elizabeth sat whimpering near the door, their hair a mess, their faces undone. King Tilus sat at the head of the table. His puffy red face looked full of steam. Prince Davien stood next to his father, surrounded by several guards and Cenaya's father.

Even watching the Efreet escape, Cenaya hadn't realized what it would mean to those left behind.

"We've searched Shelltown," one guard reported. "It's abandoned."

"Check the harbor!" the king roared. "Scour

the land! They couldn't have gone far. They will pay severely! Did anyone see anything?"

Another guard glanced back at Cenaya before taking a timid step forward. "I saw Princess Cenaya coming into the aviary in the light of the orange moon," he spoke slowly. "Perhaps she saw something."

Prince Davien scrunched his eyebrows. "Why were you out so late and on your own?"

The bite in his voice startled Cenaya. He'd never spoken harshly to her. She slid her arm with her bracelets behind her back.

"Did you see anything?" he demanded.

"No! I didn't see anything. I just went out . . ."

"I took her on a flight to give her a respite from the castle," her father insisted. "We didn't see any sign of the Efreet. We need to begin the search. They will already be difficult to find."

Prince Davien eyed her father suspiciously. King Tilus looked equally doubtful. Neither questioned him.

"You heard my commander," the king ordered.

"Move quickly. The Efreet must be found."

"Yes, Father." The prince stormed off. The guards followed.

Cenaya looked to her father as he passed her. She hoped he could read the gratitude in her eyes.

Cenaya peeked out from under her thick quilt. Leaving her curtain open at night gave her light in the morning, but it let in the early winter chill. A woodpile waited for her beside the fireplace. Piles of dirty clothes grew daily. She frowned. Her room looked clean compared to the rest of the castle. The royal family barely put their trash in a basket. They never took it outside. The stench often overpowered her.

A small hairy rodent with featherless wings screeched over Cenaya's head. Rolling out of bed, she grabbed her bow and an ordinary arrow. She pinned it to the wall just as it landed. She'd now killed two in one week. Cringing, she threw the critter in her waste basket and slumped back onto her bed. The Efreet deserved to be free. She wouldn't want it any other way, but it'd only been a couple of weeks and the castle was falling apart.

Someone knocked firmly on her door.

Pulling her robe around her shoulders, she opened it enough to see her visitor but hide her room.

"Good morning, beautiful." Even with tired eyes and wrinkled clothes, Prince Davien looked handsome.

Cenaya smoothed her tangled hair. "Good morning!"

"I owe you dinner, and I need to get out of this castle," the prince grinned. "Meet me in the aviary at sunset?"

"I'd love that." Cenaya leaned against the door. His smile melted her heart.

"Until tonight, then." He bowed before her. "Dress warmly."

♦ The Alamist Queen ♦

Wishington sparkled behind Cenaya and Talia. Prince Davien glided beside them, encircled by his blue mist. "This is all so beautiful. Where are we going?"

"Paradise!" Prince Davien's eyes twinkled. "And may I say, you look ravishing tonight."

"Oh." Cenaya felt herself blush. "Thank you." She brushed the fur cloak covering her purple dress. She'd tried to look nice, but the mess and lack of servants at the castle made that difficult.

"My father has made an arrangement with the peasants." Prince Davien's comment pulled her thoughts back to him. "It'll cost the kingdom a small fortune." His face tightened. "But starting next week we will have help again."

"That's marvelous! I was ready to start cleaning the castle myself."

"We shouldn't have to do it ourselves!" Prince Davien's eyes flashed with anger. "Someday the Efreet will pay for this treachery with their lives!"

Cenaya cowered slightly. This side of the prince scared her. She'd seen it several times since the escape, and she didn't like it. "That's awfully harsh, isn't it?"

Prince Davien sneered at her. "You've been the least upset about their disappearance. Are you sure you don't know anything about it?"

"Of course not!" she answered too quickly. "I already told the guards." She tried to sound calmer, more believable. "I didn't see anything when flying with my father."

"Yes, you did say that." His face softened, slightly. "Maybe it's because you're so kind and sensitive. Let's not talk about the Efreet." He smiled, but his eyes still looked cold. "We're almost there. I have a very special night planned. Let's not spoil it." Darting in front of Talia, he motioned for Cenaya to follow.

Cenaya nudged Talia forward. The prince moved faster. She chased after him and almost reached him. He spun around her, then paused. She rushed at him. He shot down out of the sky. Cenaya grinned and dove after him, relishing the chase. It'd been weeks since she'd relaxed and had fun.

A building fashioned after a daffodil appeared on the beach. They landed near the top petal. Prince Davien's mist disappeared. He slipped a bronze bit to a young man with olive skin who took Talia's reins and led her away.

Prince Davien slipped his arm around Cenaya's waist. "This way, beautiful."

A female with the lower body of a panther opened an elegant glass door etched with exquisite bouquets. Sculpted golden roses served as the handle. "Welcome back to the Garden, Prince Davien." She nodded to Cenaya. "My lady." Taking Cenaya's cloak, the huminal clapped her hands. Another peasant appeared. "Please show the prince and princess to their table."

Following their hostess upstairs, Cenaya marveled. Flowers of every size, color, and variety hung from the ceiling, wrapped around the stairwell, and adorned every corner and every table. Their table occupied a balcony overlooking the dance floor. The band of rabbit-halfling creatures from her birthday party entertained a hundred or more guests on the main floor.

The hostess pulled Cenaya's chair out for her. "What will the royal couple be drinking tonight?"

"Bluemelon juice, please." Cenaya accepted the offered seat.

"A jug of bubbler." Prince Davien sat back in his chair.

"This place is wonderful," Cenaya sighed. "Do you come here often?"

"Yes." He reached across the table and kissed her hand. "But never with such exceptional company." He played with the bracelet he'd given her with his thumb. "This looks beautiful on you."

"Thank you," Cenaya smiled. She'd made the right choice to just wear his. She'd stopped wearing Mayah's bracelet the day after the escape to avoid more suspicion.

A huminal with the lower body of a hyena brought them a tray piled high with a variety of meats.

Releasing her hand, Prince Davien sat back.

♦ The Alamist Queen ♦

"I'm sure you will find the food here divine." He pulled a drumstick from the tray and motioned to his plate.

The server piled meats onto it until it nearly overflowed, then turned to Cenaya's.

Cenaya placed her hand over her plate. "No, thank you. I don't care for meat."

The huminal nodded and walked away.

Prince Davien smiled at Cenaya. A bit of grease dripped out of the corner of his mouth. "They say the fruit is just as good."

Cenaya didn't have to wait long to find out. A different server arrived with a platter bearing a rainbow of fruits, vegetables, cheeses, and breads. Cenaya filled her plate, delighted to have her favorite fruit—a juicy blue athoe—as well as try several new foods.

Another server arrived with their drinks. He filled a mug of bubbler for Prince Davien.

Prince Davien raised his mug toward Cenaya. "To our escape from the castle! And to the best bubbler you'll find in Taycod!"

Cenaya raised her glass. "Thank you for getting me out."

For the next few moments, they enjoyed their meal and each other's company.

Prince Davien guzzled his mug and refilled it. His eyes shone. "You really should try a little bubbler."

Cenaya shook her head and smiled. "I'm happy with my juice."

"Very well, then." Prince Davien drained half of his mug. "At least we can dance."

He led Cenaya down to the dance floor. By the end of the first song, numerous young women had formed a circle around Prince Davien, edging Cenaya out. In a huff, she stepped back against the wall. He clearly enjoyed being well-known at the Garden.

Halfway through the third song, Prince Davien glanced up and grinned at Cenaya. Keeping her arms folded across her chest, she stared at him. The corners of his mouth fell. He stopped dancing and nodded to his admirers. Making his way to the band, he spoke in the bandleader's ear.

The song ended, and the bandleader addressed the dancers. "Please clear the floor for a special dance between Prince Davien and Princess Cenaya."

Everyone cleared the floor with only a few dancers grumbling. Bowing to her, the prince took Cenaya's hand. The band began playing her favorite tune. He led her in a graceful waltz. The magic she'd felt at her birthday party returned. Her anger disappeared, and she melted into his embrace.

At the end of the song, Prince Davien whispered into her ear, "Come with me, I have something special for you."

Retrieving her cloak, they walked hand in hand along the beach. The waves of the Rainbow Ocean—named for the point where the Green, Scarlet, Indigo, and Orange Seas blended together—washed against the beach. The fresh sea air relaxed her. She leaned her head against the prince's shoulder.

♦ Scrolls of Zndaria ♦

Around a bend in the beach, a bonfire blazed. A blanket next to the fire held a bottle of sparkling juice and two fine crystal glasses. A rhino huminal stood beside the fire. Prince Davien passed him a silver bit, and he lumbered away.

"Have you enjoyed our evening?" Prince Davien helped Cenaya sit on the blanket. He popped open the bottle and filled their glasses.

Cenaya took her juice. "It's been delightful! Thank you very much."

Prince Davien raised his glass. "A toast to the most beautiful princess." He clinked his glass to hers, then sipped from his.

Cenaya took a drink. Setting her glass aside, she reached inside her cloak. "With all the confusion at the castle, we didn't celebrate your birthday, but I bought you a gift." She withdrew the dagger she'd purchased at the Lamp and held it toward him.

"A dagger?" Prince Davien sneered. "I have lots of daggers."

"It's special," she stammered. "It—"

"I have a better gift in mind." Prince Davien tossed the dagger onto the blanket. He pulled Cenaya to him and kissed her, hard. His breath stank of bubbler.

She pushed him away. "What are you doing?"

"Showing you what I want for my birthday." He pulled her toward him again.

Cenaya pushed against his chest and stood up. "I think it's time for me to leave."

Jumping up, he blocked her path. "No one walks away from the future king!" He shot wind out of his hands, knocking Cenaya back to the ground.

Cenaya kicked him in the groin.

He fell to the blanket with a groan.

Grabbing the dagger, Cenaya bolted down the beach. Tears streamed down her face. First her father and now Prince Davien. Was there anyone in her life she could still trust?

Chapter Fourteen

A FATHER'S SECRET

Standing on her balcony, Cenaya closed her eyes and let the warm summer sun soak into her skin. In that moment, her life felt perfect again. She inhaled the fresh air deeply, relishing the peacefulness. Her stomach grumbled.

Sighing, she stepped back into her bedroom and pulled the balcony doors closed behind her. If she waited long enough, most of the royal family would be finished before she went for breakfast.

She still loved her princess sisters but found their company less enjoyable since the Efreet's escape. She knew she'd changed. Everyone else did as well. Several times, her sisters had accused her of being just like Kathlyn. She accepted that as a compliment.

Cenaya paused at the dining hall entrance. She forced herself to smile and walked around the corner. The king took little notice of her. The queen peered up out of the corner of her eye. Prince Davien looked up from his meal to glare at her. Seven months after their date at the Garden, his greeting to her remained the same.

She noticed his eyes fell on her wrist. She moved it slightly in front of her. She'd stopped wearing the prince's bracelet as soon as she arrived home from their date. Several months later, she started wearing the one from Mayah. No one noticed it or questioned her. The only attention her bracelet received was when the prince noticed it wasn't his.

Taking her seat, Cenaya met her father's gaze.

Pushing his nearly empty plate away, he rose from the table. He stopped by Cenaya's side just as a servant brought her a fresh plate. "Princess, the Creator requests your attendance at dinner this evening."

Cenaya cringed. The more she learned of the Creator's methods of bringing peace to the land, the less she wanted to be near him. She glanced around the table. The king and prince didn't look up, but they tilted their heads in her direction. Cenaya spoke softly, "Is it required?" She dreaded the answer she knew she'd receive.

"Dress in formal attire." He walked away as stoic as usual.

Cenaya's footsteps echoed with her father's as they passed the royal portraits. She mulled over questions that had haunted her since the night of the beast's attack. She hadn't spoken to him since it happened. How would he react if she asked? Would he tell her any more than he already had?

"Father?" She wrung her hands together. "Why did the Creator have the beast kill those men?" She bit her lip. "And why did you do it?"

His shoulders tensed. "When the Creator gives an order, I follow it." He didn't look at her. "Their deaths furthered his peace in Zndaria."

She'd expected his vagueness. She hadn't expected smothering silence to follow. "Have I angered you, Father?"

Stopping in front of the Creator's life-sized portrait, he faced her and rested his hand on her shoulder. "No, My Princess. I'm bothered by the Creator's actions tonight." He shook his head slowly and lowered his eyes. "I've kept a secret from you, Cenaya. The Creator intends to unveil it. You may be angry with me, but I didn't mean to hurt you." He chanted toward the painting and then spoke to her, "I promise to explain more when the time is right."

Following her father down the spiral staircase, Cenaya's stomach churned. A secret? With what little she knew about him, mystery already shrouded his life. Why did the Creator feel it necessary to divulge this particular secret? She gripped the railing to steady herself. Each answer she received left her more confused. She wanted to run away.

Passing through the shimmering mirror, Cenaya tensed. Last time, she'd feared the unknown. This time, she dreaded facing the Creator and his creatures. The rust-skinned monsters silently eyed their movements. A flicker across the door confirmed a shadow warrior awaited their arrival. The door swung open, and the warrior showed them into the ballroom.

The bronze statues, marble busts, and fine paintings remained unchanged from her first visit. One thing differed. In the center of the room, five padded chairs surrounded a table set with fine plates and crystal goblets.

The Creator rose from his seat next to his seer stone. "Thank you for joining us, Cenaya." He took her hand and bowed slightly. "You look stunning. Truly fit to be the Alamist Queen."

Cenaya shuddered under the Creator's praise. She hadn't tried to please him or look extravagant. Her gown flowed freely to her ankles. The sleeves stopped just below her elbows. It fulfilled the requirement of formal attire without Cenaya feeling as if she were celebrating.

"And your father looks ready to lead my army into our new world."

Cenaya's stomach lurched at the mention of the Creator's new world, but she couldn't deny that her father looked regal. His fitted burgundy tunic with gold trim and matching cape differed greatly from his usual breastplate. Her father glared at the Creator.

If the Creator noticed, he didn't show it. Touching Cenaya's elbow lightly, he escorted them to the dining table.

She glanced back at her father. She'd never seen him speak ill of the Creator or treat him with disrespect. What would the Creator reveal tonight that caused his anger?

Soft footsteps approached from within the Creator's cavern.

The Creator smiled. "It appears our other guests have arrived."

Watching the entrance, Cenaya held her breath. The fletcher, Eva, entered the room. An ivory and brown band circling her head perfectly complemented her dark-brown hooped gown. A young boy in a tunic grasped her hand. He looked more nervous than Cenaya felt. The horns protruding from his dark slicked-back hair and his rusty skin matched the fletcher's appearance. His purple eyes darted around the room. The fletcher's eyes moved between the Creator and Cenaya's father.

Cenaya exhaled slowly. She glanced from her father to the child and back to her father.

The Creator waved to the chairs across from him. "Eva, it's good to see you and Gabriel again." He pulled a chair out for Cenaya. "You remember our young princess, Cenaya, correct?"

"Of course," the fletcher smiled sweetly at

Cenaya. She helped Gabriel into a chair. His feet dangled at least a boot-length above the ground. "It's wonderful to see you again, my dear."

Cenaya's father held a chair for the fletcher, pushing hers in at the same time the Creator pushed in Cenaya's. He took the seat between Cenaya and Eva. Only the Creator looked comfortable.

Taking his seat between Cenaya and Gabriel, the Creator clapped his hands. "Princess, thank you for joining us for Gabriel's birthday." A rust-skinned monster placed an elegantly wrapped box on the table next to the young child. "I can't think of anyone more appropriate to attend."

The young boy looked at the fletcher. With her encouragement and assistance, he lifted the lid. His eyes widened as he lifted a golden breastplate from the box. "Thank you, sir," the boy spoke timidly.

The Creator grinned. "You're very welcome, Gabriel. Do you recognize it, Cenaya?"

"Yes, of course." Cenaya nodded. "It matches

mine and my father's."

"And it will protect Gabriel just as yours protects you." The Creator clapped his hands again. "I hope everyone enjoys the meal."

Three monsters appeared and placed crisp salads drizzled with a fiery red dressing in front of the guests. The Creator took the first bite. Cenaya glanced around the table. The others had started eating. She took a bite. The dressing contained a spice new to her. It warmed her mouth with an intense peppery taste, then immediately cooled it with a distinct peppermint flavor. In a more comfortable situation, she would've loved it. Finishing her salad, she laid her fork on her plate about the same time as the others.

The Creator clapped. The monsters returned, replacing their salads with bowls of burgundy soup. As with the salad, Cenaya would've loved the unique spicy flavor in a different setting. They finished their soup, and he clapped again.

This time, the monsters replaced their empty dishes with wooden bowls. Steam wafted from an eggy bread mixture. Everyone's, except Cenaya's, was topped with dark cubes. Cenaya's first taste melted in her mouth.

"Do you like it, Princess?" the Creator asked.

Cenaya jumped slightly at the break in the silence. She nodded, swallowing her second bite. "Yes, very much, thank you."

"It was prepared specifically for you. The other plates include my favorite food." The Creator lifted a cube on his fork. "Dragon bits." He chewed the bit slowly and swallowed, smiling contently. "But I knew you wouldn't enjoy that." He set his fork down. "I know and care about you, Cenaya. I know the food you eat." He waved to the plate in front of her. "And I know how much you love your family. That is why I invited you to dinner."

Cenaya followed the Creator's eyes to her father. He stared at the Creator, his lips straight, his jaw tight.

The Creator raised his eyebrows. "Will you tell her, or shall I?"

Turning to face her, her father's expression

softened. "Cenaya," his voice caught, "I loved your mother very much, but I was drawn to the power the Creator promised me. Several years after I joined him, I realized my life was hollow, but it was too late." He grasped Cenaya's hand. "I couldn't rejoin you and your mother without drawing you into the Creator's world, and I refused to do that." He pushed his plate away and leaned on the table. "Not long after that, I met Eva." He locked eyes with the fletcher. "We filled a void for each other and soon fell in love." Eva smiled tenderly. He looked back at Cenaya. "Shortly before you arrived here, we married." He looked across the table. "Gabriel is my son." He turned back to Cenaya with watery eyes. "Gabriel is your brother."

Cenaya looked around the table. The Creator ate his meal freely. He seemed relaxed, satisfied even. Looking bewildered, Gabriel glanced between his mother, his father, and Cenaya. Both the fletcher and Cenaya's father watched her carefully.

♦ The Alamist Queen ♦

"Why didn't you tell me?" Her calm voice surprised her, hiding her stirring emotions. "How could you keep this a secret?"

She looked up at her father. He held her gaze briefly, then dropped his eyes. "I'd planned on telling you later, when the time was right."

"You should have told me when I first arrived!" Cenaya jumped up and escaped onto the balcony.

Of all his secrets, how could he keep this one? Taking deep breaths, she tried to make sense of everything. Not only did he abandon her and her mother, he moved on and started a new family. Then, he kept it a secret until the Creator threatened to tell her first.

Leaning against the balcony railing, she felt as fiery as the lavafall spilling into the shimmering lake. The valley was beautiful, just like before, but this time, it was empty.

The door opened behind her. She straightened up, ready to confront her father.

"I'm sorry I upset you, Cenaya." The Creator's voice made her cringe. She turned to him. His soft expression didn't match the smirk in his eyes. "I felt you needed to know."

Cenaya wouldn't discuss her family with him. "Where's your army?" She looked over the quiet valley.

The Creator stepped up beside her. His sickening grin now matched his eyes. "They're continuing to fulfill my dream of a new world."

Cenaya bit the inside of her lip to stop her reaction. She detested how he spoke of peace but exercised violence.

"You belong with me, Princess, with your family." He placed his arm around her shoulders. "As beautiful as the underworld is, Eva and Gabriel long to roam freely in your world." He leaned closer to her. "Once you become the Alamist Queen, my plan will be fulfilled. With peace throughout Zndaria, Eva and Gabriel will no longer be trapped in the underworld. They will join you and your father. You'll be a family. Isn't family the most important thing in life?"

"Of course," Cenaya whispered, suppressing a

shudder. She now understood why her father had kept the secret, and why the Creator chose to reveal it.

"Let's return to the celebration." He turned her away from the valley. "My chef has prepared a chocolateberry truffle for dessert."

Cenaya didn't resist and reentered the dining hall with the Creator. She was no longer confused. She was terrified.

Chapter Fifteen

THE GOLDEN WIZARD

Cenaya woke to a nudge on her shoulder and sat up with a start. Her father stood over her. The hood of his black cloak lay on his back. His pegasus stood just outside the open balcony doors, bathed in purple moonlight. A summer breeze warmed the air. She hadn't been asleep very long. "Father, what are you doing here?"

"I'm going to battle." He knelt beside her. "Please listen carefully. This is the first time I've been able to speak freely. The Creator is leading his army against the Halls of Magic. This is one of the few moments I know he's not watching either of us."

Cenaya shuddered. She hated the constant watching, the violence in the name of peace. Everything about the Creator bothered her. She shifted to face her father.

His deep purple eyes bore into hers. "Let there be no doubt, the Creator is pure evil."

"I know, father. I feel it whenever I'm around him. So . . ." she hesitated. "Why do you serve him? Surely there's a way for you and your family to escape."

"When I joined the Creator, I tied my life to him." He hung his head. "Even if Eva and Gabriel escaped, I could not."

"But father—"

He held up his hand. "Please, listen. My life is set, but yours is not." His eyes glistened. "You must leave at dawn."

"What?" She recoiled. "But what about the

Creator's attack on Meredith? We'll know if mother is alive."

"The day you met the Creator, I told you you'd have to make a difficult decision. This is it. If you don't leave, you may forever be under the Creator's control. The Creator told you he plans to attack the Swamp Witch, yet we've never discussed it in our war strategies. When I've asked about it, he simply states it will be when the time is right."

"What are you saying?" She stood up. "He promised me he would reunite us if she was still alive."

"Since you joined us in Taycod, the Creator has been preparing you to become the Alamist Queen. It would be easier for him to make you the new queen than to convince your mother to join him. I don't know this for certain, but I know the Creator's ways. If you don't attack Meredith, we may never know the truth about your mother."

"*Me* attack Meredith?" Cenaya slumped back onto her bed. "How could I possibly do that? Even if I could, the Creator would find me in his stone before I'm out of Taycod."

Her father lifted her chin with his finger. "I wouldn't send you off without a plan. At daybreak, visit the wizard, Wynslow. He doesn't support King Tilus's tyranny." He stood and paced the floor. "Once he casts the deflection spell on you, the Creator won't be able to watch you in the seer stone. As for the attack on Meredith, help awaits you at Eastern Island. They can help you free our people from the Troll Dungeon."

"Our people have been slaves in the Troll Dungeon?" The thought sickened her. "Is mother there?"

"My sources could only confirm that our people were imprisoned. There was no sign of your mother. You must determine if she is still alive when you attack Meredith." He placed his hand on her shoulder. "Then, the Alamist must be used to stop the Creator."

She placed her hand over his. It'd been less

than two weeks since she learned about Gabriel. She was still angry with him but understood the risk he was taking coming to her tonight. "What will happen to you when he is stopped? What will happen to Eva and Gabriel?"

"I don't know. I've done many things of which I'm ashamed. I must answer for them someday." He gripped her shoulders. "But you can't worry about that or about Eva and Gabriel. This is the reason I didn't tell you about them sooner. You must do what is best for Zndaria and your future without letting thoughts of us cloud your judgment. Do you understand?"

"Yes, Father."

He handed her a quiver of arrows. "These are from Eva. They're the same ones you made with her before. You'll need them in your attack."

Memories of making her arrows lifted her spirits some. "Thank you, Father. I'll do my best."

He kissed her forehead. "Travel safely, My Princess." She followed him to the balcony. Mounting Nightmare, he turned to her once more.

"You have my love, Cenaya."

Cenaya watched him disappear into the darkness. For most of the ten years since she'd arrived in Taycod, she'd hardly gotten to know him. Within the past few months, she'd learned more about him than she wanted to know. Yet, he was her father, and it pained her they were being separated once again.

She walked into her closet. What did she need to take? She shoved several outfits into her knapsack. It filled quickly, and she still didn't feel ready to leave. It was happening too fast. She leaned back against the wall and slid to the floor. Blinking back tears, she looked around her closet.

This had been her home for so long. She had to leave, that was certain, but could she do it alone? She didn't stay behind when the Efreet left expecting to be in this situation. She thought of Kathlyn who'd never shown weakness, not even in front of the king. What would she do right now?

Cenaya took a deep breath and rose. Emptying her knapsack on the floor, she started over. Changing into her armor, she placed her nightgown and a few reasonable outfits, including the brown dress from Kathlyn, into her bag. From her dresser, she needed her hairbrush and a couple of clips. She slipped Mayah's bracelet onto her wrist. Everything else could stay.

She cinched her bag closed and looked around her room one last time. The dagger she'd purchased for Prince Davien sat on the closet shelf. Kathlyn would definitely take that. Cenaya strapped it to her ankle. Now she was ready.

Stepping again to the balcony, she sighed. The orange moon overhead meant it was only halfway through the night. She couldn't visit Wynslow until morning, but waiting here would drive her mad. She snuck into the kitchen for a few provisions before sliding open the aviary door. Making her way to the stall, she saddled Talia and slipped the food into her saddlebag.

"Isn't it a little late for a flight?"

Cenaya whirled around.

Prince Davien's tight face matched his accusing voice. "I suppose you're going for another flight with your father."

"What I do is none of your concern." She folded her arms over her chest. "Why are you here?"

"The guards alerted me to the light in your room. It appears the Creator was correct to have us keep an eye on you tonight."

"Since when do you serve the Creator directly?"

Prince Davien grabbed her hand. "Since he promised you'll be my wife. Once you're the Alamist Queen, we'll rule side by side. Or at least, that's how it'll appear," he sneered. "You'll control the Alamist, and I'll control you."

Cenaya tried to pull her hand away. His grip caused Mayah's bracelet to dig into her wrist. "I'll die before I marry you!"

"Fear not, my dear." His snide sentiment cut her like a knife. "I won't let anything or anyone harm you. We will be married and because you willingly submit to the Creator, your father's new family won't be harmed either."

Cenaya's shoulders drooped. The Creator told her about Eva and Gabriel to use them against her. Her thoughts raced. She knew what she had to do. "I don't have a choice, do I?"

Prince Davien smirked. "That's a much better attitude for my wife." He loosened his grip.

She threw her elbow into his jaw and bolted from the aviary. Talia's stall slammed shut behind her. Guards in the courtyard cut off her escape.

Prince Davien approached, rubbing his jaw. "That was very foolish, Princess," he spat out her title. He slapped her across the cheek. She stood tall, ignoring the pain. "If you try that again, your princess sisters will also pay the price." He lifted his hand as if to strike her again.

"Lamra—Tsho—Eco—Xiasar!" Bright light filled the air.

Cenaya tried to look behind her. She couldn't

turn her head. Only able to move her eyes, she glanced at Prince Davien. He and the guards also stood frozen in place.

A lanky young man on a three-headed beast landed in front of her. His tousled golden hair touched the golden cloak around his shoulders. The monstrous animal had the body of a lion, giant eagle wings, and the tail of a scorpion. Its three heads—bear, wolf, and bull—growled at Prince Davien and his raised hand. The prince's eyes widened.

"We need to leave before the spell wears off." The young man touched his glowing staff to Cenaya's shoulders, breaking the spell on her.

Cenaya caught her balance. "Who are you?"

"I'll explain after we're gone." He offered her his hand. "Do you need to ride with me, Princess?"

Cenaya looked at Prince Davien. Anger flared in his eyes. If this young man wanted to hurt her, he wouldn't have stopped the prince. "No." She rushed into the stable and flew out on Talia.

The young man led her over the castle walls. The turret guards nearest the aviary also stood frozen. Others rushed toward them, but not in time to stop them.

When they were a safe distance from the castle, the young man turned over his shoulder. "I'm Nathanial McGray, the Golden Wizard of Versii, but you can call me Nate."

"Nate?" She studied him closer. He looked familiar. "Are you the boy from the Crossroads Inn?"

The corner of Nate's lips turned up. "I wondered if you'd remember me. We never got a chance to thank you for your help or see if you were alright. How did you get out of there so quickly?"

"My father had already retrieved our animals. He wasted no time getting me back to the castle." Her mind flashed back to her father and the Creator standing over her in the recovery room. "If you're from the Crossroads Inn, then is your friend . . ." She didn't finish the sentence. Right now wasn't the time to ask if his friend was the boy the beast had killed. "What were you doing in the courtyard?"

"We need your help to defeat King Siddon. I was supposed to meet Sir Kilnipy at the castle tomorrow. I just arrived tonight and wanted to figure out where I was going before I found a place to stay. When I saw what was going on, I had to help. Maybe we can make it to the Halls before Sir Kilnipy leaves in the morning."

"Thank you for your help." She shuddered at the thought of the prince's hand raised at her. She would've found a way out but didn't know how. "Wait!" She pulled back on Talia's reins slightly. "You said 'the Halls.' Do you mean the Halls of Magic?"

Nate slowed to look back at her again. "Yes, of course."

She felt sick. "We can't go there. My father told me to escape just before he headed there to join the Creator in his attack."

"Who's the Creator?" Nate asked, but then

shook his head. "That's not important right now. If they're under attack, we have to help them. Come on, Demon." He nudged his creature and bolted away from Cenaya.

Cenaya caught up to him. "I've seen the Creator's army. You'll be helpless against it. Besides, my father didn't help me escape so I'd go straight to the Creator."

"My friends are there. I have to try. Are you coming or not?"

She looked back at the castle, then down at the town. The Creator didn't expect them to be there. Could they surprise him and help the people at the Halls? She couldn't see Nate ahead of her. He was headed to the Halls with or without her. In the time since she'd met the Creator, she'd felt helpless to stop his violence. She nudged Talia forward, and they darted to catch up with Nate. She didn't know what she could do, but she wouldn't just sit by and watch the Creator's evil plans progress.

Chapter Sixteen

THE HALLS OF MAGIC

Nate guided Demon over a side path veering off the main road. The Halls of Magic should have been visible. Instead he saw a dark cloud. He glanced behind, hoping to see Cenaya. With a sigh, he accepted his reality. He had to do this alone. Pulling out his staff, he pushed Demon harder.

The dark mist thickened and a familiar chill enveloped them. Nate had expected to face the same army he'd fought at the White Castle earlier that month. But there was no army. There was only destruction. The once stunning blue crystal Halls of Magic lay in rubble.

Nate's hands shook. He guided Demon toward the wreckage. His stomach lurched. Bloody harpies, imps, griffins, and gremlins filled the moat. A lava dragon lay motionless—half in the water, half on the bank. He flew above the rubble, desperate for any sign of survivors. Where were all his friends, especially his girlfriend, Loretta?

Crumbled white stone—the remains of the statues of the Hall's founders—dotted the blue crystal. He landed beside the now crinkled, ripped banner that once circled the founders' statue in the garden. A mix of sadness and anger surged through him. The Halls existed to increase wisdom by embracing differences. Why would anyone want to destroy that?

Someone gasped nearby. Nate ran to the sound. A gremlin lay under a chunk of crystal.

"Andia—Molas—Afay." Nate levitated the

♦ The Alamist Queen ♦

crystal and tossed it aside. He recognized the gremlin immediately. Captain Galo lay in a pool of blood. Gashes covered his body and face. Nate dug the healing potion from his knapsack.

Captain Galo coughed. Blood spurted from his mouth. "Nathanial?" He inhaled sharply. "We fought bravely, but—"

Nate put his hand on the gremlin's shoulder. "Drink this first." He placed three drops into Captain Galo's mouth.

Clenching his jaw, the gremlin swallowed the hot liquid. His wounds began healing. "Thank you, Nathanial." He sat up slowly. "My strength is returning."

Nate sat beside him. "What happened?"

Captain Galo sighed. "We fought valiantly through the night but never gained the advantage. When dawn broke, Master Loperian had to surrender or everyone would've been destroyed. All the survivors were taken in there." He nodded to smoldering rocks some distance from the Halls.

♦ Scrolls of Zndaria ♦

Nate mounted Demon, then pulled Captain Galo up behind him. Circling the area, Nate stared in dismay. A jagged black ring of upheaved earth surrounded a dark tunnel leading underground. Any vegetation remaining around the hole lay charred or withered. "What could've done this?"

"Only pure evil," Captain Galo insisted. "Unlike anything I've seen before."

"Do you hear that?" Nate looked around.

Captain Galo nodded.

Faint singing floated from across the crater. A fresh grey stem stood a few boot-lengths tall among the blackened brush. The singing continued. Nate pushed Demon forward. The stem grew higher. Several soft violet leaves unfurled. Five glimmering silver petals stretched into a glorious blossom.

Nate had seen a flower like that only one other time. Sliding off Demon before they landed, he rushed to the woman—Blinkly's mother—singing weakly beside the flower. An arrow protruded from her back. Blood soaked the front of her dress. Her chest heaved with each breath. Her pale skin wrinkled around her sunken, closed eyes. She looked much older than she had when he'd left for the Halls of Magic less than a year ago. Nate choked back tears at the sight of his best friend's mother so close to death.

Kneeling beside her, he lifted her clammy, worn hand in his and stroked her grey-streaked hair. "Lady Gordenall?"

Her once vibrant eyes fluttered open. "Nathanial, I thought I heard your voice." She coughed. "I'd hoped to see you once more before I joined my dear Danzandorian."

Despite their situation, Nate smiled softly at the sound of Blinkly's given name. "I can help you." He lifted the healing potion to her mouth. Captain Galo stood ready to remove the arrow.

A lion's roar echoed within the tunnel. She clutched her wound and gasped, "He's returning!" She gripped Nate's arm with her free hand. "Danzandorian swore he could stop Siddon." Her breaths quickened. King Siddon led three Mistriders out of the tunnel. They all rode black lions. Lady Gordenall's eyes darted toward them. "He mustn't learn my true identity!" She lay back, pressing the arrow to the side. More blood seeped from her torso. Nate watched helplessly. "Find the secret to the medallion!" She released her grip on Nate. Her body fell limp against the charred vegetation.

Raging, Nate jumped to his feet. He yanked his staff from Demon's saddle. First, he'd lost Blinkly. Now, he couldn't save Blinkly's mother. Twenty boot-lengths in front of him, the elf who'd started the war on Zndaria and destroyed Blinkly's family strutted smugly toward them.

"F-F-Fal." Nate paused just long enough to gain control. He wouldn't fail Blinkly again. "Falma—Ottsa—Omstrafa!" Lightning shot from his staff.

King Siddon swept his cloak in front of him. It absorbed the lightning.

Nate seethed. "Falma—Ottsa—Omstrafa!"

Once again, lightning shot from the staff.

King Siddon blocked the spell a second time. "You're wasting your time, boy," he sneered. "Where is the princess?"

"I came alone," Nate spat. "She said it was too dangerous."

"Oh, but you're wrong," King Siddon smirked. "The foolish girl is coming and when she arrives, she'll join you and the others in the underworld."

A ball of energy shot out of King Siddon's hand. Nate felt a shove from behind and fell to the ground. A dark cloud engulfed Captain Galo. When it cleared, Captain Galo was gone.

Nate leapt to his feet. "Tsho—Hysha—Raza—Kilna!" Icicles rained down on King Siddon and the Mistriders. The elves merely swept their cloaks over themselves and their lions. They stood unharmed and unamused.

King Siddon cackled, "You're a mere boy. You can't beat us. We will destroy you and everyone else who stands in our way." Spreading his arms wide, he jeered, "Just as we've done here." He moved his lion forward. "You've seen the destruction we've already caused," he smirked. "Imagine what we'll do when we control the Alam—"

An arrow struck the ground at King Siddon's feet. Bursting into flames, it created a blazing wall between Nate and the Riders. Nate looked up. Cenaya turned and began flying away. Nate sighed with relief. She'd come to help him after all. Demon barked at Nate. Nate jumped on his back. Demon flew away from the flames, away from King Siddon. Cenaya kept her distance ahead of them.

"Stop him!" King Siddon bellowed below.

Nate glanced back to see the Riders emerge from the wall of flames with their cloaks draped around themselves and their lions.

King Siddon shot a ball of energy at Nate. Demon jerked out of the way just in time. He shot again, but they were out of his range. "I will find you and the princess!" His voice faded behind them.

♦ The Alamist Queen ♦

Catching up with Cenaya, Nate glanced back one more time. He could barely make out the ruins of the Halls. He'd never forget them. The Creator had captured his friends. He had to save them, but how? Even with help from Cenaya—even if they had an army—how could they defeat the man who'd conquered Master Loperian and destroyed the Halls of Magic?

Chapter Seventeen

RELEASE

Nate flew behind Cenaya in silence. He glanced over his shoulder many times, making sure they weren't being followed, struggling to believe the Halls had been destroyed. Cenaya glanced around more than he did. The dark mist around them cleared. It felt like they were far enough away to be safe.

Nate pushed Demon to fly beside the princess. "Thank you for coming."

"You're welcome." She shifted in her saddle. "I'm sorry we couldn't do more to save your friends."

Images of those from the Halls of Magic flashed through his mind. "I didn't think you were coming, but King Siddon was expecting you. How did he know?"

"The Creator watches me in his seer stone." She cringed. "I'm sure he searched for me as soon as he found out I was missing."

"Watches you?" Nate looked around again. "Does that mean he could be watching you right now?"

"It's very likely." Cenaya frowned. "We have to make it back to Wishington to visit the wizard, or I'll never be free from him."

"But, if they were waiting for you at the Halls, they're sure to be waiting for you in Wishington."

"I know," she sighed. "But he has to cast the deflection spell over me." She nudged Talia forward. "I don't have a choice."

"Maybe you do." Nate guided Demon

downward. "Follow me."

Landing at the edge of a clearing, Nate pulled a worn, leather-bound book from his knapsack. "This is the Red Wizard's spell book." He flipped through the pages. "He might have a deflection spell in here."

Cenaya bit her lip and glanced around. "If this works, it'll be better than returning to Wishington."

Nate studied a page near the back of the book. "I found it. I need to cast the spell on an object you'll always have with you."

Cenaya glanced over her body. Her eyes stopped at her wrist. "My bracelet from Mayah will be perfect." Slipping it off her wrist, she handed it to Nate. "What will the spell do to it?"

Nate placed it on a rock. "It will illuminate it." He glanced at the spell book one more time, then touched the bracelet with his staff. "Danfor—Alfa—Motas—Taham—Qatz."

Nothing happened.

Nate rubbed his chin. "That can't be right." He

scanned the page. He'd said one word wrong.

Cenaya shifted from one foot to the other. "Maybe it won't work, and we should head back." She rubbed her arms. "We don't have much time."

"I can do this. Give me one more try."

Cenaya wrung her hands together but nodded.

Nate practiced the spell under his breath several times. Resting his staff against the bracelet again, he took a deep breath. He spoke slowly, emphasizing each word. "Danfor—Alfa—Molas—Taham—Qatz."

Light shot out of the staff, washing over the bracelet. The once dull white shells shimmered in the sun. Nate picked up the bracelet. Lines of color flashed across each shell. He handed it to Cenaya.

"Thank you!" She slipped it back on her wrist.

Nate looked into the clearing behind her. He'd been here before. His feet felt frozen, rooted to the ground. His chest tightened. He struggled to breathe.

"What's wrong, Nate?"

Forcing one foot in front of the other, he staggered into the clearing. "It's this place." His voiced sounded far away. He felt as if he were in a trance.

"Nate?"

Nate looked around the clearing. His eyes stopped on a certain tree. Rage, despair, and distress surged inside him. He wanted to run, to release the energy, but he could barely move. "This is where Blinkly died," he whispered.

"Blinkly? Your friend from the Crossroads Inn?" Cenaya's voice was just louder than Nate's. "How . . . did he die?"

"A beast." Nate's anger surfaced. He clenched his fists. "A savage, horrifying beast!" He stomped over to a blue boulder just large enough to encase a withered old man, resisting the urge to kick it. "And this is him!"

Cenaya stared at the boulder. "This is what happened to the old man?"

Nate spun around to fully face her. "How do

you know about the old man?"

She stepped back. "My father . . ." she hesitated. "My father delivered him to the escort party. He . . . he said it was his purpose."

"Your father?" Nate sputtered. "Blinkly is dead because of your father?"

"I'm so sorry." Her voice broke. "But I'm also at fault. I . . . I could've stopped him. I had the chance to kill the beast, but I assumed he wouldn't make it. I still can't imagine how he survived his injuries."

Scenes from that night flashed through Nate's mind—the beast pushing dirt over their fire . . . Blinkly trying to control it . . . Nate stumbling over the spell . . . Blinkly using his dagger against the monster, then being thrown into a tree . . . the same scenes that often haunted his sleep. Knowing that one man placed the beast in their path enraged him. Knowing he held the final blame for his best friend's death cut into his heart. Despair overtook his anger.

"The beast would've died." Nate's legs folded

underneath him. "But Blinkly and I healed him." He looked up. "We found the old man nearly dead and gave him some healing potion. He attacked us later that night. Blinkly died because I stuttered and couldn't cast a spell fast enough." A tear ran down Nate's face. "Blinkly died because of me."

Cenaya sat down beside him. "I don't think it would've ended even if either of us had stopped the old man. The Creator was intent on killing your friend. If it hadn't been the beast, he would've found another way."

Nate wiped his cheek. "Who is this Creator you keep talking about?"

"He's my father's master and the one behind the war on Zndaria. He also controls King Siddon and the others. He promises to build a better world but does so through force and deceit. He wants me to become the Alamist Queen to further his conquest." Cenaya shuddered. "But why was your friend a threat to him?"

Nate pulled the medallion from under his

shirt. He traced the handle of the mighty war hammer engraved into the gold with his finger, stopping at the massive ruby that formed the hammer's head. "Because he had this—the key to stopping the war."

Cenaya touched the ruby. "How can a medallion stop the war?"

"I don't know." Nate let it fall against his chest. "All I know is that Blinkly swore he could stop Siddon and that the medallion holds a secret. His mother didn't have time to tell me anything else before she died."

"My mother will know." Cenaya's eyes shone. She rose to her knees. "Once we rescue her, she'll know what to ask the Alamist. She can help us fight against the Creator!"

Nate stood and helped her to her feet. "That's great, but we can't do it alone. The Halls are destroyed. We'll have to go back to Burrowville for an army to help us."

Cenaya mounted Talia. "I have help waiting for me. We need to get to Eastern Island."

♦ Scrolls of Zndaria ♦

Nate climbed onto Demon and flew after her. She'd trusted him. Now he needed to trust her.

Chapter Eighteen

EASTERN ISLAND

Cenaya led Nate over the Rainbow Ocean. Moonlight shown off the swirling waters. A cluster of islands appeared in the distance.

Demon lunged forward, pulling at Nate's hold on the reins. His bull head bellowed, his wolf head yapped, and his bear head roared.

Nate tightened his grip. "I've never seen him like this before. Who did you say lives on this island?"

♦ Scrolls of Zndaria ♦

"The Druid Empress rules Eastern Island," Cenaya spoke over Demon's exclamations. "My father told me I'd find the help I needed there."

They flew past the northernmost island, the home Cenaya left as a child. She fought back a tinge of homesickness. She'd return someday.

Faint bellows, barks, and roars answered Demon's exclamations. Before long, numerous creatures came into view. Druids in hooded robes flew on the backs of winged bears, wolves, and bulls, all of which greeted them with excitement that matched Demon's. The creatures surrounded them.

One of the Druid riders locked eyes with Demon and bowed. "Welcome home, Your Highness."

Demon barked as if in response.

"The empress eagerly awaits your arrival," the Druid said.

Cenaya looked to Nate. He'd never said anything about Demon being royalty. Nate looked equally surprised.

Demon pulled ahead of Cenaya and led the party to Eastern Island while exchanging yaps and barks with the other flying animals.

They approached a towering mountain dotted with clusters of trees. A river running along walls of moss-covered stones encircled it. Demon led them directly toward the hillside. A wall of shrubs parted, providing a landing area for the guests.

It felt very familiar to Cenaya. Talia trotted after Demon down a grassy corridor. Draping vines provided perches for colorful-breasted birds singing a harmonious melody. They entered a great hall where the vines continued the natural décor. Cenaya looked around, trying to place the memory. She'd been here before, but when?

A woman with nearly shaven red hair sat on a throne adorned with brightly colored flowers. Her forest-green robe complemented her smooth olive skin. She rose to embrace Demon as Nate slid off him.

"Lord Vala! I'm elated by your homecoming. Your mother has been most distressed by your extended absence."

Demon yapped in response.

"Did you fancy your excursions throughout Zndaria?"

Demon bellowed and then barked gently.

The empress nodded. "Indubitably, young prince, virtue and vice abound in all places. Who have you escorted to our beautiful island?"

Demon barked again and nodded at Nate.

Nate bowed to the empress.

"Welcome to Eastern Island, Nathanial McGray. I recall you from the council at the Halls of Magic. My son, Bylo, speaks highly of you."

Nate looked ready to speak. Before he could, Demon yapped and nodded at Cenaya.

Gasping, the empress stepped to Cenaya and ran her fingers along one of Cenaya's braids. "Is it you, child?" She choked on the words.

Warmth filled Cenaya's chest. Why did this woman seem so familiar? "I'm Cenaya, Princess of the Alamist. Thank you for welcoming us to your island."

The empress threw her arms around Cenaya. "Dear child! I've wondered about your whereabouts since the attack on your kingdom." The empress stepped back and cupped Cenaya's face in her hands. "Knowledge of your safety brings me much elation! Do you recall your previous tarriances to our island?"

Cenaya shook her head. *So I have been here before!*

"Your mother and you ventured here frequently." The empress smiled warmly. "And what of your mother? I've had no tidings from her since the attack."

Tears filled Cenaya's eyes. "I have no news of my mother, but my father has instructed me to find her."

"Your father?"

"Yes, my mother sent me to him once she knew she couldn't escape. He has cared for me in Wishington since then. He's learned that my people are captive in the Troll Dungeon. I'm to free them, then attack the Swamp Witch to find my mother."

"How dreadful for your people! Imprisoned in that abominable dungeon all this time. We shall deliver them at once."

"Thank you, Your Majesty. The news Nate received at the Halls of Magic makes it more important than ever."

"You tarried at the Halls?" A smile filled the empress's face. "Did you see my Bylo?"

Cenaya hung her head.

The empress's smile faded. "What of the Halls?"

Cenaya looked at Nate.

Nate stepped forward. "Your Majesty, unfortunately, the Halls are destroyed." He swallowed hard. "Those who survived were taken prisoner into the underworld."

The empress stepped back and dropped to her throne. "The Halls are destroyed? How is that conceivable?" She covered her mouth with her hand. "My dear Bylo! I inquire again, did you see my Bylo?"

"Not among the fallen, Your Majesty," Nate said softly. "I believe he was taken prisoner with the others."

The empress sat quietly. Cenaya watched her among the room's silent observers. The heartbreak of losing a family member pressed heavily on her.

The empress stood slowly and stroked Demon's mane. "Young prince, your mother anxiously awaits your return. Go at once."

Demon nuzzled her hand with his bear head, then growled lowly. He started out of the ballroom with the other flying bears, wolves, and bulls following behind. They moved somberly, their previous excitement taking on the despair in the room.

The empress placed her hand on Cenaya's and Nate's shoulders. "We must contact the Council immediately. They must know of the Halls." She moved to the milky stone beside her throne and chanted.

The stone began to swirl. Cenaya moved closer

♦ Scrolls of Zndaria ♦

to the table, intrigued as faces appeared in the stone until they covered the surface.

"Thank you all for convening so rapidly," the empress addressed the Council. "Nathanial McGray and Princess Cenaya arrived in my kingdom today with dreadful news. The Halls of Magic have been destroyed. Master Loperian and many others have been taken prisoner. I shall let Nathanial impart the details to you."

Nate stepped forward, bowing slightly to the Council. He nodded to the face of a man with straight red hair within the stone.

"Last night, I asked Princess Cenaya to join our alliance. As we were leaving Wishington, she told me of a planned attacked on the Halls. We left immediately but arrived too late." Nate's eyes moved among the faces in the stone. "After I healed Captain Galo, he told me the battle lasted all night before Master Loperian felt the need to surrender." He stopped speaking and seemed to stare into the stone before continuing. "Sadaki?"

The face of an elderly man with dark skin

enlarged in the stone. His gold embroidered cap sat straight on his head. "I'm Sadaki's father," his voice wavered. "Was he among the fallen at the Halls?"

"My apologies, sir, your son bears a strong resemblance to you, sir." Nate bowed slightly again. "I didn't see him among the dead. I believe he was taken prisoner with the others."

First relief, then dread washed over the man's face. Cenaya shared his pain. All the talk of attacks and prisoners made her own painful memories surface.

"Lady Gordenall also survived the attack." Nate cleared his throat. "I offered her the healing potion, but when she heard King Siddon returning, she rushed to speak and didn't drink it. We, I . . ." Nate barely spoke. "I didn't arrive in time to save her." He paused. "She died before we could help her escape." Nate's head drooped. "I'm sorry I failed her and the others."

"My boy." The red-haired man's face enlarged in the stone. Pain filled his eyes. "If Master

♦ Scrolls of Zndaria ♦

Loperian felt the need to surrender, you would've been captured as well. I'm grateful you escaped unharmed."

"Thank you, sir." Nate met his eyes. "But I still would've been captured if not for Cenaya. King Siddon killed Captain Galo. Cenaya knew he was there on the Creator's command and made sure I escaped."

"Who is this Creator of whom you speak?" the Red Wizard asked.

"I just learned about him today from Cenaya." Nate turned. "Cenaya, this is the Red Wizard."

The Red Wizard bowed to Cenaya. "It is my pleasure to meet you, Princess. Thank you for your service to Nathanial. We felt you'd be a treasured ally to our fight, and you've already proven that to be true. Please tell us more of this Creator."

Cenaya stepped forward. "The Creator is the man behind the war on Zndaria." Her voice felt timid. She wasn't used to being the one everyone listened to. All the faces in the stone and room watched her. She cleared her throat. "Including my father, there are five individuals in his Court. They all seemed to come from different lands. He speaks of peace and creating a world where everyone will exist together without fear." Her heart felt heavy. "But he accomplishes his goals through violence and death.

"Last night, my father told me I must escape if I didn't want to join the Creator. He believes the Creator plans to force me to become the Alamist Queen. The attack on the Halls provided the distraction needed for my escape." She looked at the Druid Empress.

The empress addressed the Council again. "It appears Cenaya's father contrived a strategy for her. He discovered her people are imprisoned in the Troll Dungeon. We shall negotiate their freedom. If the trolls demur, we shall liberate them. Many of you have consigned aid throughout Zndaria. Could any of you bestow more?"

Most of the Council members shook their

heads.

"Your Highness." The face of an aged treeman grew in the stone. "I understand the importance of freeing the princess's people. But if this Creator destroyed the Halls of Magic, how can any of us expect to fight him?"

An extremely wrinkled woman's face eclipsed the treeman. "I was at the battle in Burrowville. Nathanial found a way to win that battle. We can't win the war alone, but we *can* win it." She looked at the empress. "I have faith in your cause. I only wish we could spare troops to aid you."

The Red Wizard's face grew again. "As you are aware, most of the kingdoms have sent all whom they can spare to retake MaDrone and defend Versii. I'll discuss your situation with King Darwin. Perhaps we can send a few of our warriors to your aid."

The empress nodded. "The assistance would be greatly esteemed. Thank you again for convening rapidly. We shall conclude this council until further information is procured."

The faces in the stone nodded and vanished one by one until all Council members had left. The milky stone settled.

Cenaya faced the empress. Could they succeed in their mission even though some on the Council doubted them? "Your Highness, are we going forward foolishly?"

"Fear not, my child." The empress led Cenaya and Nate to the side of the great hall. "If our attempts at negotiation fail, the addition of Versii's warriors shall be sufficient."

She touched the wall. The vines parted, and the stone slid open to reveal a set of granite stairs. Cenaya and Nate exchanged questioning glances but followed the empress in silence. Passing through an archway, they entered a training room three times the size of the great hall filled with stone targets and obstacles.

Cenaya stared in amazement. Covered in armor and blasting targets with fireballs, her Efreet friends masterfully used their powers that had been forbidden in Taycod. Encircled in red smoke, they flew through the air, looking ready for battle. Mayah and Kathlyn rushed to Cenaya at the same time.

Shooting out of the sky, Kathlyn embraced her first. "I knew you'd join us someday! I'm so glad you're here!"

Mayah pulled on Cenaya's sleeve.

Cenaya scooped her up in an embrace. "Mayah, you're using your powers!"

"Yes!" Mayah beamed. "We've all been training so we can help you."

Cenaya set Mayah down. The rest of the Efreet encircled them. "Help me?"

Haze grinned. "We're prepared to fight for you, Princess."

Cenaya smiled, first at the empress, then at the throng of Efreet. She couldn't have hoped for a better army. It was time to free her people and save her mother.

Chapter Nineteen

THE TROLL DUNGEON

Cenaya guided Talia onto the beach on the northern tip of the trolls' island. The sticky summer air hung around them. Bright red flowers among thick leaves in the surrounding brush looked much cheerier than she felt. Nate landed beside her. Haze on the mule dragon and a band of Druids on their beasts followed and moved to the cover of the brush.

Cenaya turned to Haze. "You know the plan. If

♦ Scrolls of Zndaria ♦

we don't return by midday, get the army and come after us."

"We won't wait a moment longer." Haze slid off the dragon. "I don't trust the trolls."

"Neither do we. But maybe their love of gold will get them to work with us." Nate padded one of his four saddle bags. Two more bags were tied to Talia, each full of gold bits.

"Besides," Cenaya sighed, "we expect them to betray us. We just need to know that my people are alive." She directed Talia up a dirt path. "Are you ready, Nate?"

Nate nudged Demon into the air. Flying over the dense forest, knots twisted in Cenaya's stomach. She'd have to act confident when they reached the dungeon, but the unknown nearly unnerved her. They passed over steep barren terrain which led them to a stone arch. The deep canyon below the natural bridge appeared more inviting than the dungeon on the opposite side.

Carved into the granite mountainside, a massive iron door provided the only entrance to

♦ The Alamist Queen ♦

the windowless dungeon. No one had ever escaped this impenetrable prison, allowing the trolls to charge exorbitant amounts to hold prisoners for other kingdoms. A sentence worse than death, the Troll Dungeon was the ultimate punishment.

Sliding off Talia, Cenaya heaved an iron ball hinged to the door. She dropped the ball with a boom that echoed throughout the canyon. Looking nearly straight up to see the top of the prison, she shuddered. Her people had suffered here for so long. The echoes faded.

Nate stretched his neck. Cenaya fiddled with the arrows in her quiver. Demon and Talia pawed at the ground. They had no choice but to wait. They weren't leaving until they were seen. Suddenly, a piercing screech broke the silence. A thin slit in the iron door opened several boot-lengths above Nate.

"Visitors are not welcome!" The troll's gruff voice made the words sound even less inviting.

"We're not visitors." Cenaya stared up to the

troll's dark, hairy eyes to feel stronger. "I've come to buy my people's freedom."

"We don't release prisoners." The troll slammed the slit closed.

"I'll pay ten times the price the Swamp Witch paid you to hold them!"

The slit reopened slowly. "This is highly unusual." He grunted. "Wait here while I get the dungeon master." He closed the slit. His heavy footsteps faded away.

They waited longer this time. Cenaya resisted the urge to pace. The troll had sounded confused and hungry for gold at the same time. They might work with them. Then again, she reached for her bow, they didn't know what to expect. She caught Nate's eye. "Be ready for anything."

He lifted his staff already gripped by his side.

The iron gate creaked and ground open. Trolls filled the dungeon courtyard three rows deep. Standing several boot-lengths taller than Nate, they held long iron spears next to their bulky, leather-clad frames. Scowling, they looked ready to attack on command.

Cenaya and Nate lifted their weapons, ready to defend themselves. Demon leapt in front of them, scorpion tail in strike position, heads roaring.

"Call off your beast!" The sea of guards parted for a shorter, unarmed troll dragged down by his pot belly. His shoulders slouched forward.

"Demon, stop!" Nate said.

Demon flew up in the sky, hovering closely over them.

"That's much better," the short troll sneered through crooked, decaying teeth. "Did you expect the dungeon master to meet you without an army and his wizard?"

The lanky, elderly troll behind the dungeon master jeered at Nate and Cenaya. Tusks protruded from his cheeks and wrapped toward his ears. A skull rested on the end of his staff.

The dungeon master stepped forward. "And who are you?"

"I'm Cenaya, Princess of the Alamist. This is Nathanial McGray, the Golden Wizard of Versii.

We've come to buy my people's freedom."

"Step forward, child," the dungeon master commanded.

Cenaya stepped up to the gate. Standing eye level with her, the dungeon master grabbed her chin with his hairy hand. He moved her head from side to side. "Yes, you look just like your beautiful mother."

Cenaya resisted cringing from his touch and putrid breath. His mention of her mother made her heart race.

Releasing his grip, he stared into her eyes. "Why would I bargain with you? It wouldn't be good for my business if I released prisoners."

"Had the Council known you held innocent people in your dungeon, they would've taken action to free them. Instead, I'm here to buy them. I'll pay you ten times the price Meredith paid to keep them here. Gold is better for your business than a battle."

The dungeon master rubbed his chin. "You make a strong argument, but ten times is an insult. It would take triple that for me to consider such a bargain. How do I know you can pay?"

"I have six bags with me." Cenaya stared back into his black eyes. They widened noticeably. *Good, I've got his attention.* "I will give you this gold now in exchange for some of the prisoners and return for the rest."

"You silly girl! Meredith paid a fortune. Your gold doesn't fully pay for even one prisoner. But in a show of my trust, I will fetch one for you."

The dungeon master turned. The guards once again parted. He stopped in the rear and addressed two guards. "Fetch the old woman!"

The guards closed off. The troll wizard glared at Cenaya and Nate.

They stood firm in their silence. Demon landed beside Nate, glowering at the trolls, ready to attack. Talia whinnied and scuffed her hooves against the hillside.

Finally, the sea of guards parted. The dungeon master dragged an elderly elf with rough skin and purple hair behind him by the shackles around her wrists. She stumbled over the chains on her ankles. Her ragged clothes hung loosely from her thin frame.

The dungeon master gripped her arm. "Here is one of your precious people."

Cenaya gaped at the woman. Despite her rough appearance, her toned arms showed years of hard work. She stood with dignity even in chains. Cenaya couldn't maintain her firm stance. She stepped forward, reaching toward her former handmaiden. "Prevesa?"

Tears streamed down the elf's cheeks. "Princess? You're alive? I thought I'd never see—"

"Enough!" The dungeon master yanked Prevesa's shackles.

She fell to her knees and cried out in pain.

"Give me the gold!"

Cenaya's fire returned. "How do I know you'll keep your word and free my people? Allow Prevesa to come to me first."

"You do not order the dungeon master. Give me the gold!"

♦ The Alamist Queen ♦

Cenaya knew she didn't have a choice. She nodded to Nate.

"Andia—Molas—Afay!" Nate tapped the four saddle bags on Demon and the two on Talia with his staff. He raised his staff in the air, and the bags followed. They floated through the iron gate.

"Now release Prevesa!" Cenaya ordered.

The dungeon master waved at his wizard.

"Distafay—Nala." The troll wizard waved his staff at the iron gates. They banged shut, separating Cenaya and Nate from the trolls, and from Prevesa. Nate jerked, losing control of his spell. Thunderous clanging sounded from within the courtyard.

"No!" Cenaya banged on the gate. "Prevesa!"

"I don't release prisoners," the dungeon master's muted voice penetrated the wall. "Now be gone!"

Cenaya yanked a black arrow from her quiver.

Nate caught her arm. "Not now, there are too many of them. We need to stick to the plan."

Cenaya replaced the arrow. Her reasoning

returned, but her anger remained. Yes, they had expected betrayal. She mounted Talia. But she hadn't expected to see Prevesa, for her to be so close to freedom. Glancing back at the gate, she nudged Talia into the air with Nate right behind her. "Let's get to the others. We have to find a way to free her."

They flew back faster than they'd come. It felt as if Talia shared Cenaya's anger. They landed in the clearing and were immediately surrounded by Haze and the Druids.

"They took the gold and refused to release any prisoners!" Cenaya slid off Talia. "They have my childhood handmaiden, but we couldn't find out how many more. If the others are like her, they're overworked and undernourished."

"What of the dungeon?" Haze pressed.

"We couldn't learn much," Nate explained. "It's carved into the mountain with no windows. An iron gate four boot-lengths thick appears to be the only entrance through a wall covering the courtyard."

"We couldn't learn about the inside . . ." Cenaya stared into the forest and rubbed her eyes. Was she really seeing this?

Two young men ran through the forest—away from the dungeon. One, dressed all in black, continually glanced behind him. The other's pale skin contrasted sharply to his companion. His eyes darted around them. Just as they reached the clearing, they bolted for the beach.

Cenaya shot an arrow directly in front of them. Rushing toward them, she heard the others follow. The arrow transformed into a sandstorm, scooped up the runaways, and deposited them at Cenaya's feet.

The Druids surrounded them before they could recover. They rose slowly.

Cenaya notched another arrow in her bow. "Who are you, and how did you get here?"

The taller, pale man faced Cenaya. His shoulders relaxed. His red glowing eyes against his pale skin revealed him as Undead.

A chill ran through Cenaya. She shook it off. "I

asked you a question!"

The shorter one jabbed him with his elbow. "Don't say anything!"

The Undead shrugged. "We just escaped."

"Escaped?" Cenaya lowered her bow slightly. "From the dungeon?"

The Undead nodded.

"Then you have a choice. Help us free my people, or we hand you back to the trolls."

Chapter Twenty

UNLIKELY ALLIES

Nate stared at the two fugitives. They looked rough. Gashes marked the Undead's pale face and arms. A dark bruise cradling the other's eye nearly matched his clothing. A bloody scratch across the side of his face stood out against several scars. Both reeked of the dung clinging to them from head to toe.

The guards surrounded them.

Cenaya held her bow ready. "You didn't tell us

who you are."

The pale one stood tall and didn't take his eyes off Cenaya's. "I'm Odran, and he's Tadeas."

Nate recognized a knapsack on the ground behind them. His mother had given it to him to take to the Halls of Magic. A thief stole it after attacking Nate and Blinkly at the Crimson City docks. "You!" He pointed his staff at Tadeas. "You're the one who stole my bag!"

Tadeas shrugged his shoulders. "So what if I did? You made it easy." He talked as if he didn't care, but his eyes darted around the guards.

The guards tightened their circle around him.

Haze moved closer and ignited his hands. "Don't even think about running."

"Andia—Molas—Afay." Levitating the bag to him, Nate dug through it. Of course, most of his things were gone. Mingled within the thief's belongings, he found his now flat coin bag and a half-empty fat jar with a thin neck. Nate yanked it out of the bag. "You drank some of the invisibility potion?"

The thief laughed uneasily. "Trust me, you don't want to touch that stuff. It really messed me up!"

Nate shoved the potion back in the bag. "That's because it would only work for Blinkly and me." He flung the pack over his shoulder. "If we'd had it when we were attacked by the beast, Blinkly might still be alive." He clenched his fists.

Cenaya stepped between Nate and Tadeas. "We don't have time for this, Nate!"

"She's right." Odran stepped in front of Tadeas. "It's just a matter of time until the guards figure out how we escaped and secure it."

"Oh, no!" Tadeas shook his head. "I'm never going back in there. Just give me my things, and I'll be on my way."

Nate glared at the thief. "This bag is mine, and now, so is everything in it. You'll get your things after we've made it out of the dungeon safely."

Cenaya nodded at Odran. "We'll discuss our plan on the way." They both started into the forest.

Nate turned to Tadeas. "Are you coming, or should we tie you to a tree?"

Tadeas glanced around at the guards. Haze's flames were out, but he stood ready to defend. "Fine," he sighed. "I'll get you inside, but then you're on your own. I'm not dying for anyone."

The Druid guards and Haze prodded Tadeas forward. Nate and Demon joined Cenaya and Odran to devise a plan. At the edge of the forest, Nate moved the healing potion from his pack into one of his pants pockets and jammed the invisibility potion from his newly found knapsack into the other pocket. Placing his cloak inside his pack, he secured both bags onto Demon.

He looked to the guards. "He doesn't touch this pack unless he's with us."

"Yes, sir." The head guard nodded to Nate, then turned to Cenaya. "We'll see you before nightfall, or we'll return with an army to free you."

"Thank you." Cenaya stroked Talia's mane, then handed her reins to the guard. "Let's move out."

Nate dropped a step behind Tadeas, keeping his staff pointed at Tadeas's back. Following Cenaya, Odran, and Haze, they rushed through the barren expanse along a steadily flowing muddy stream. Near the stone mountain, the stream became darker and thicker. A stench filled the air.

Cenaya covered her nose with the crook of her arm. "What's that smell?"

Tadeas smirked. "It's the dungeon sewer." They stopped at a hole in the base of the granite mountain just large enough for one of them to duck through. "And it's your way in."

Nate glanced at Odran. Tadeas couldn't be serious.

Odran grinned. "It's minimally guarded. We just had to wait for a distraction and you provided the perfect one."

"Let's get moving." Tadeas pushed past them. "I don't want to spend any more time with you than I have to." He stooped through the hole,

◆ Scrolls of Zndaria ◆

then stuck his head back out and looked at Haze. "Oh, and if Fire Hands even thinks of lighting up, this whole place will explode." He disappeared into the darkness.

Nate ducked in after him with the others right behind. The smell overwhelmed him. Gagging several times, he covered his nose with his arm. "Maloh—Octama." He held his illuminated staff in front of him. If he reached his arms out in any direction, he'd touch the walls or ceiling of the shallow tunnel. He trudged forward, following Tadeas through the murky, lumpy stream. Glancing down, Nate wished he couldn't see it.

The group stepped into a cavern. Dung filled what should've been a clear pool. Water trickled from a hole only a few boot-lengths across directly above the dung heap. A rope hanging from the opening dangled just out of their reach.

"This is as far as we can go." Tadeas crossed his arms over his chest. "Unless the weak-stomached wizard can get you up there, I'll lead the way back to get my things." He started back out the cavern.

"Not so fast. Andia—Molas—Afay!" Nate caught Haze in the spell. Relishing Tadeas's look of dismay, Nate levitated Haze to the rope and then aimed his staff at Cenaya.

"Send me next." Odran moved in front of her. "I'll help him secure the room."

"Why should we trust you?" Cenaya asked.

"Because if you fools mess this up, you'll be imprisoned," Tadeas spat. "We'll be executed."

"Besides," Odran continued, "I know the dungeon and how the guards operate."

Cenaya nodded to Nate.

"Andia—Molas—Afay." He lifted Odran to the rope just as Haze disappeared through the opening.

Odran scurried up the rope. To Nate's surprise, he truly seemed to want to help them.

"You're next. Andia—Molas—Afay." Nate lifted Tadeas to the rope. Odran had already vanished through the opening. Once Tadeas made it up, he lifted Cenaya, then took a deep breath. He'd never tried levitating himself. He wished he knew a better spell, but this would have to work.

Moving his hands to the top of the staff, he pointed it at his chest. "Andia—Molas—Afay!"

Tilting the staff upward, his feet lifted off the ground. He glanced down. *It's working! I'm levitating myself! I'm ...* His wandering thoughts broke the spell. He fell to the ground.

Razzle! He glanced up at the hole to the dungeon. He had to get up there.

Casting the spell again, he kept his eyes on the tip of the staff. He repeated the words in his mind while continually tipping the staff upward. Wobbling, he followed the dangling rope. He slowly raised himself through the hole in the ceiling, stepping into a room twice as big as the cavern. The same horrific stench hung in the air. Cenaya grabbed Nate's elbow and steadied him.

Two troughs running the length of each side of the room slanted toward the opening in the floor. Holes in the walls aligned above them. Numerous shovels, scrapers, and brooms leaned against the granite. Two hairy trolls sat slumped against the wall behind Odran and Haze.

Nate peered past them. "What happened to the trolls?"

"Odran knocked them out just before they tore me apart." Haze rolled his shoulders. "I'm glad he's on our side."

Odran moved toward Nate away from the unconscious trolls. He seemed embarrassed by the praise. "We need to move forward with the plan. Are you ready, Nate?"

Nate worked the invisibility potion from his pocket. "How'd you find this place?"

"When the sewage gets backed up, a prisoner is assigned to drudgery. The guards dole it out as punishment." Odran grinned at Tadeas. "We were chosen a lot."

Nate cringed. Could there be a worse job?

"We didn't have to be geniuses to see the escape route," Tadeas chimed in. "Let's get this over with."

Nate uncorked the bottle. When he'd watched

the alchemist use unicorn dung to create the potion, he'd hoped never to use it. Now he stood in the dungeon sewer ready to drink it. How fitting. To distract himself, he pictured a room full of chocolateberry treats—pies, pudding, cake, cider. He lifted the bottle to his mouth and gulped.

As soon as it hit his stomach, he felt queasy. His head spun. He flinched, feeling as if he were walking through thorny brush. And then, it all stopped. His hand holding the bottle glowed. No, his whole body glowed!

Everyone in the room stared at him.

"You're invisible," Cenaya gasped.

Tadeas reached out to touch him. "Whoa! That's not what happened when I drank it!" His eyes shifted. "But you can still see your staff." His regular personality had returned. "I'll hold it for you."

Nate slapped his hand away. "I don't think so!" He handed the staff to Cenaya. "You have a different job."

"Fine." The thief pulled his hood over his face. "Follow me."

He led Nate up several levels of steep steps. Nearing the main floor, they heard footsteps and flattened themselves against the wall. Two troll guards stopped at the head of the stairs and sniffed in their direction. Nate held his breath.

"The drudge must be backed up again," one troll growled to the other.

Nate glanced at the dung coating Tadeas. At least he proved helpful for one thing.

"Let's get the scrawny thief." The trolls lumbered away.

Tadeas nudged Nate and motioned to stairs across the entrance. "The wizard's room is on the second floor at the end of the hallway on your left. Make it fast," he hissed. "They're about to find out I'm gone."

Nate glanced back down the stairs. He didn't have long before the others would join Tadeas. He had to distract the troll wizard before then. He darted past two doors that opened to the courtyard. Six nearly full bags of gold—the one's they'd brought with them—sat on the granite floor.

"Finish picking up that gold and get it to the vault," the dungeon master barked.

Nate grinned. At least the trolls had to work for the stolen gold. He bounded up the stairs two at a time, then rushed down a short hallway to a stone door. Holding his breath, he eased it open. He relaxed only slightly when it didn't creak. Inside, an orb spinning slowly in the air cast light on a plush bed, numerous paintings, and marble floor. The room contrasted surprisingly to what Nate had seen of the rest of the dungeon.

The troll wizard looked up from his seer stone and sniffed toward the door. He took a step away, but his head snapped back to the stone. "What are they doing in the dungeon?" His gruff voice matched his annoyance. He reached for his staff.

Nate pointed his hands at the wizard. "Tsho—Hysha—Oglog—Pinz!" Ice shot out of his palms, striking the back of the troll's head.

♦ The Alamist Queen ♦

Cursing, the troll whipped around. His head crystallized. The ice spread to the wizard's feet, rooting him to the floor.

"Pinz—Pesi." Nate stopped the spell. He turned his attention to the seer stone. Cenaya, Ordan, and Haze had reached the top of the dungeon stairs. He rushed through already open doors onto the wizard's balcony.

The dungeon master looked up from the courtyard, eyeing the wizard's room suspiciously. Several trolls hefted the heavy bags of gold toward the entry.

Nate pointed at a bag of gold. "Falma—Ottsa—Omstrafa."

Lightning struck the bag, splitting it open and showering gold into the courtyard. The troll carrying the bag stopped abruptly. The trolls behind him slammed into him and each other. He held up the split bag and looked confused.

"You fool!" the dungeon master berated him. "Clean this up immediately!"

Nate shot lightning at two more bags. Gold

covered the courtyard. Trolls rushed to pick it up.

"You blundering idiots!" The dungeon master smacked a nearby troll on the back of the neck.

"Ota—Esta—Nocafa." Nate blasted the courtyard with a gust of wind, blowing the gold bits out of the guards' reach each time they tried to scoop up a pile.

The dungeon master kicked the nearest guard. "You imbeciles! How hard is it to pick up gold!"

"Alza—Ontra—Hera—Jira." A dark blob formed in Nate's hands. He flung it at the troll he'd first hit with the lightning spell.

Growing as it flew, the bubble engulfed the unsuspecting troll in a tar ball. It bounced along the ground, sucking up gold bits in its path. Another guard ran to help and was sucked into the ever-growing trap. A third guard ran to their assistance.

"Stay clear of the blob!" the dungeon master ordered. The rest of the guards moved to the corner opposite the bubble. The dungeon master looked around frantically. "What madness is happening here?"

"Alza—Ontra—Hera—Jira." Another tar bubble started forming in Nate's hand. The dungeon master looked up. Nate grinned. *This one's for you.*

"There!" The dungeon master pointed in Nate's direction. "Hit the orb!"

Nate glanced down at the blob he held. It didn't glow like the rest of his body. Suddenly, pain seared through his arm. A hand axe clanged to the floor beside him. Another troll in the courtyard threw an axe at Nate. It buzzed by his ear. He grabbed his arm and ducked away from the window. The bubble fell to the floor. A spear passed through the window where he'd just been standing. Blood gushed from his wound. The blob bounced around the room until it sucked up the frozen troll.

"To the wizard's room!" the dungeon master bellowed.

Nate forced himself to his feet. He took only two steps before he collapsed. Blood surged from his arm, painting the floor red. He gasped in pain. He fumbled in his pocket for the healing potion. Using his good hand, he uncorked the bottle. He lost his grip on it. The potion spilled out on the floor. Scooping it up, he tilted the bottle to his mouth. He could only hope. A single drop fell out. It wasn't enough.

Footsteps sounded outside the door. He could crawl past the guards, but how long would he last? He pushed himself onto his knees. He had to try. The door swung open.

"Nate?" Relief washed over Nate at the sound of Odran's voice. "Nate, we have to leave."

Nate slumped back to the floor. "Over here." He waved the empty healing potion bottle in the air. "I need help. My arm is cut badly, and the guards are coming."

Odran lifted Nate in his arms with ease. He rushed to the door and toward a loud commotion downstairs.

Nate forced his eyes to stay open. They reached the entrance. Striking with the cleaning tools from the drudge, Cenaya's people fought against the trolls with the strength of caged animals. They outnumbered the trolls in the entrance three to one. Nate couldn't see the dungeon master. They subdued the trolls, either knocking them out or binding them together.

Odran rushed Haze and handed Nate to him. Blood stained his already dirty clothing. "Get him to safety. I'll find Tadeas and make sure no one follows you."

"No!" several elves protested. "You have to come with us!"

"I'll meet up with you soon. Go with the princess."

Cenaya watched the exchange. "You've befriended my people?"

Odran shrugged, "Yes."

Cenaya reached down to her ankle. "Will this help you?" She handed him a dagger.

"Absolutely!" Odran's eyes widened. "But how—"

A grinding noise echoed deep within the

dungeon. Fierce roaring followed.

Odran took the dagger from Cenaya. "Get Nate to a handmaiden." He ushered them out the main gate. "I'll take care of things in here."

The group rushed through the courtyard where only a short time earlier they'd been betrayed. Nate grimaced in pain. Cenaya released a high-pitched whistle. The flyers would come for them. They'd get off the island. Nate sighed and closed his eyes. Whatever happened to him, at least Cenaya's people were finally free.

Chapter Twenty-One

THE PRINCESS'S ARMY

Nate opened his eyes. He lay on a bed of woven leaves. Glistening vines covered the ceiling, lighting the room. He propped himself up on his arms. Clean robes replaced his clothing soiled in the dungeon. The table next to him held bowls of herbs and a variety of tools. It looked very similar to the Halls of Magic infirmary. Memories of his time there after being attacked by the shadow warrior flashed through his mind.

♦ Scrolls of Zndaria ♦

"How's my patient feeling?" a familiar voice floated from the doorway. Nate's sister entered wearing a frock covered with pockets. The belt secured around her waist held several pouches. Her strawberry-blonde hair sat atop her head, twisted into a bun.

"Denya?" Nate sat up completely. "What are you doing here?"

"I brought her." A stockier version of Nate burst into the room. Dressed in dark-blue armor with a rapid-fire crossbow holstered on each side and the hilt of a long sword extended over his shoulder, Ted looked ready for battle. His golden hair—although shorter than Nate's—brown eyes, and large nose showed the family resemblance. "The Red Wizard sent the best ta help. So, of course we're here."

Nate could only stare. He'd never expected both his brother and sister to be fighting with him.

"Besides," Ted broke the silence, "ya keep getting yerself inta trouble. If I can't keep ya safe, she has ta put ya back together."

Denya lifted Nate's shirt sleeve and unwrapped his bandage. "You're looking at the head handmaiden for Ted's battalion," she said with pride. She removed the tight yumber leaves, smeared a cream over the well-healing wound, and replaced the bandage.

Nate moved his arm. It barely hurt. "How long was I out?"

"Long enough." Ted threw away the old bandage for Denya. "We were coming ta finally wake ya up."

"A little over a week." Denya rolled her eyes at Ted. "I gave you herbs to keep you asleep to help your arm heal." She wiped the cream from her hands on a rag. "But we were coming to wake you. The armies are gathering and the empress has asked for you. Do you feel well enough to come with us?"

"Of course!" Nate swung his legs off the bed.

Denya placed her hand on his shoulder. "Slowly, you've been down for a while."

♦ Scrolls of Zndaria ♦

They walked down a hallway similar to the other corridors in the castle. Chirping birds filled hanging vines. A bubbling stream flowed beside the walkway. Denya and Ted chatted, but Nate's thoughts wandered. He wasn't in pain, but his head felt foggy. He remembered leaving the trolls' island with the others but nothing after that. Is that when he blacked out? The stream turned under a wooden bridge and poured out of the castle. How many of Cenaya's people were they able to free? Could their army succeed in an attack against the Swamp Witch?

At the end of the hallway, they entered an oversized crate. A Druid secured a gate behind them and gripped a set of ropes. Another Druid grasped a different set. Together, they lowered the contraption.

Descending within the mountain, Nate brushed his hand against the exposed soil. "How many warriors came with you?"

"Most of the army is tryin' ta retake MaDrone," Ted explained. They passed an opening. "We could only spare a few of us now ta help plan the attack, but the Red Wizard will send more as the time draws near."

They passed another opening. Nate rubbed his arm. "I'm glad you're here, Denya, but if you're the battalion's head handmaiden, why did they send you ahead instead of keeping you with the battalion?"

"We didn't know how many of Cenaya's people would need care so I came to assist the Druids." She ruffled Nate's hair. "And when I heard my baby brother needed help, I wanted to be right there."

Another opening passed. Nate pushed her hand away but smiled. If felt good to have them all together again, even though it'd only been a few weeks since he'd seen them.

They passed several more openings before coming to a stop. The three McGrays followed the Druids out of the contraption and through a drape of leafy vines into the training room. Here, thousands of Efreet and Druid warriors worked together seamlessly. It was clear they'd spent many months training together. Sprinkled among them, Cenaya's people wore garb from the Druids instead of rags. No longer dull, their skin had regained its glow.

Nate eyed the gathering in awe. "If I hadn't helped free them," Nate marveled, "I wouldn't believe Cenaya's people had spent the last ten years in a dungeon."

"Yes," Denya smiled. "They've responded well to our treatments."

Cenaya stood with Haze, Kathlyn, and the Druid empress overseeing the training. She caught Nate's eye and waved them over. Many warriors in the room parted for them to walk through.

"Nathanial." The empress stepped forward and embraced him. "I'm elated by your expeditious recovery."

"Thank you, Your Majesty." Nate bowed slightly. "So am I."

"Your sister's healing aptitude rivals many of

♦ The Alamist Queen ♦

the elite healers in my acquaintance." She placed her arm around Denya's shoulders. Denya blushed. "And your brother's advisement on our stratagem has been most meritorious."

Ted crossed his arms over his puffed-out chest. "Just doin' my duty, ma'am."

Cenaya smiled. "And we appreciate your service." She became serious and turned to face Nate. "As part of our strategy, we need two things from you."

"Anything!" Nate answered without hesitation. "What can I do?"

"My people haven't seen my mother since they were captured. If she's alive, she must be locked in the Witch's Hut." She stepped to a table holding a parchment and pointed to a rough drawing of a cliff. "I can blow the main gate." She moved her finger to what looked like a rounded hut. "We need you to cast a spell to get Ted, you, and me past the grob army and inside."

Nate studied the parchment. "How thick is the door? And how long do I have?"

Ted stepped forward. "We think it's two, maybe three boot-lengths thick. Ya have until the rest of the army arrives in a month or so."

Nate glanced around the group. Ted acted like that was plenty of time. Wizards with years of experience trained for months to master spells like that. He exhaled slowly. He'd have to search his spell book and start right away. "What else do you need from me?"

Cenaya, Ted, and Haze looked at the empress.

"Regretfully, we lack an essential portion of our army. I believe your unique acquaintance with Lord Vala is necessary to procure it."

"Me?" This surprised him more than needing to learn a difficult spell. How could him knowing Demon help them? "What can I do?"

"Please accompany me." The empress led Nate away from the group back into the wooden contraption.

Two Druids pulled the ropes, lifting them through the castle. Nate waited for her to explain.

"Although our army is formidable, the addition

of the young prince and his siblings would prove invaluable. Unfortunately, his mother obdurately refuses the blessing for her children to join our battle. Because you liberated the prince in your land, I believe you can implore the queen to vacillate."

Several openings higher, the Druids halted the contraption, then wrapped the vines tightly to steady it. Nate followed the empress out to a wall of entwined vines.

"I shall conjoin with the queen and become a conduit betwixt the two of you. I shall be incapable of communicating with you but trust you'll prevail in this endeavor." She smiled kindly at Nate. "The queen and her children anticipate our arrival. Do you require any additional counsel?"

Nate shook his head, but he didn't know what to expect and didn't feel ready. How could he convince a queen to change her mind?

The empress ran her fingers down the vines. They untangled and parted, revealing a room nearly identical to the Druid's grand hall. Winged bears, wolves, and bulls—some hovering, some crouching—filled the hall. Staring at a three-headed creature twice the size of Demon, Nate barely noticed Demon's wolf head lick his cheek.

The empress bowed. Nate did the same.

"Your Majesty." The empress rose. Nate continued following her lead. "I present Nathanial McGray, the Golden Wizard of Versii. He is the companion who arrived with the young prince. If I may approach, he desires to beseech approval for your children to join us in battle."

The bull head of the queen bellowed. Her silver wings glistened.

The empress stepped forward and placed one hand on each of the bear and wolf heads. The eyes on all three of the queen's heads closed. The empress closed her own eyes.

"Are you the young man who saved my child?" The Druid Empress spoke, but her voice was deeper, gravelly. Her eyes had opened, but they shone yellow.

♦ The Alamist Queen ♦

Nate forced himself to address the creature not the empress. "Yes, Your Majesty. I helped a friend release Demon—I mean—Lord Vala."

"I'm eternally in your debt. He is my only heir and will someday lead all my children. His adventures in Versii were against my wishes." Demon growled softly, but she continued without addressing him. "You are here to ask me to let my children join your battle, correct?"

"Yes." Nate cleared his throat and shifted from foot to foot. "We need them to defeat the Swamp Witch, Meredith. We must learn if she holds the Alamist Queen captive."

"My children stay on this island at my request. As the prince discovered, Zndaria is full of danger. I couldn't bear to lose one of them to those dangers as I thought I'd lost my heir. Now I'm asked to send them into harm's way? Surely you can understand why my answer is no. You saved him once. I shall not tempt fate and risk his life again."

Nate felt sweat drip down his face. He glanced

at the empress for assistance, but she remained in the conduit trance. He fidgeted with his shirt collar. His hand brushed the medallion, and he gripped it for strength. "I said I helped a friend free the young prince." He pictured Blinkly's anger that day the trapper profited by letting festival-goers throw rotten tomatoes at Demon. "My friend wouldn't let someone wrong your child. Danzandorian also saw the destruction of the evil army spreading across our land first hand when they invaded his kingdom. He's dead now because the Creator was determined to kill him.

"You and your children are safe here, for now, but that won't last. I can't promise they won't be injured if they join us, but I can promise that the Creator and his Court won't stop until they've conquered all of Zndaria, including Eastern Island. We have to stand up for what's right, even if it means risking our lives."

The queen shifted between her paws.

Thinking about Blinkly gave Nate a surge of energy. "When we attack Meredith, we'll free the

♦ The Alamist Queen ♦

Alamist Queen. She'll use the Alamist to help the Council. We can't stop the Creator—can't protect this island and your family—without her. Your children can help our victory. We need them. Please, please let them join us." Drained by his emotional plea, Nate dropped his hands to his side and stood still.

None of the creatures in the room moved or made a sound. The queen didn't respond.

Demon stepped forward, grunting and growling lowly toward her. It sounded like pleading.

The empress's lips moved, but she still spoke with the queen's gravelly voice. "The young prince tells me this Danzandorian freed him because it was the right thing to do. He believes he'll be a better ruler if he can stand against the evil in the land."

Silence again.

Nate shifted from one foot to the other. It didn't feel like she'd invited a reply. He reminded himself to breathe.

"To protect the future of my people," the voice nearly whispered, "I will allow my older children to join your battle." The creature's heads drooped slightly.

Nate sensed her pain but was grateful for the blessing.

The empress blinked. She removed her hands from the queen, and the dark color of her eyes returned. Stroking the wolf's fur tenderly, she smiled gratefully at Nate.

Demon roared to his siblings.

They yapped back.

Feeling their excitement, Nate exhaled slowly and grinned. He'd completed one of the tasks asked of him. They had their army.

Chapter Twenty-Two

THE WITCH'S HUT

Cenaya guided Talia between the trees along a cliff overlooking the ocean. Nate, Ted, Haze, and Kathlyn landed with Cenaya's people and Ted's army behind her. The red moon dipped near the horizon, creating cover for them during the complete darkness just before dawn. Dismounting, she moved to the edge of the hillside. The outline of the Witch's Hut barely stood out in the blackness.

Kathlyn stepped up beside her and linked elbows with her.

"They're all following me into battle." Cenaya glanced over her shoulder. "What if it's a mistake? What if my mother's not here?"

"Then we'll have delivered a punishment that's long overdue and removed a threat to peace." Kathlyn leaned her head against Cenaya's. "And you'll have answers. Either we'll restore your mother to power or you'll become the Alamist Queen." She turned to face Cenaya. "You are ready for this. That's why we're following you. We all believe in you."

"Thank you!" She hugged Kathlyn tightly.

Orange and red streaks appeared in the sky. They stood in silence, watching the rising sun illuminate what was known through the land as the Witch's Hut. It was more of a fortress. Hundreds of spikes protruded from the outer shell. A ring of thick oak tree trunks aligned with the thick wooden gate created a barrier to the courtyard. A grassy expanse separated the hillside from the hut.

Cenaya nodded to the small army. "It's time."

Leading them down the hillside, Cenaya's feet sank slightly into the damp soil. She felt small among the massive terrain. Midway down the hill, she released a grey arrow toward the hut. It struck the ground and transformed into a stone. Barreling across the grass, it grew into a boulder and picked up speed. It struck the wooden gate, shattering it upon impact.

Ted grinned. "She knows we're here now."

A low rumble sounded from within the courtyard. Engulfed in smoke, the boulder hurled back toward them, moving faster than before.

"Look out!" Cenaya jumped out of its path.

The boulder shot through the small army. Clanging armor and grunts mixed as everyone dove to safety. A pained cry rang above the sounds. The boulder disappeared over the hill.

Pulling herself to her feet, Cenaya rubbed mud off her arms. "Is everyone alright?"

Most of the army picked themselves up, ready

to continue the battle. One archer remained on the ground, his leg noticeably misaligned.

Denya rushed to him, sliding her pouch off her shoulder from underneath her shield woven from redwood leaves. "I'll take care of him. You deal with Meredith."

Grobs poured out of the courtyard, taking their stance many rows deep. Armed with spears, maces, and shields, the leather-clad bulky swamp creatures chanted menacingly. Meredith rode to the head of the army, clutching the mane of her stallion. Just as they'd hoped, it looked like the entire army had come out to meet them.

Cenaya moved beside Nate and Ted. "Are you ready?"

Nate nodded and held his staff in front of him. Cenaya and Ted each gripped a side of it. Cenaya glanced at Ted's secured sword and crossbows. He could be using them very soon.

Haze and Kathlyn stepped forward. "So far, everything is going according to plan. You find your mother. We'll take care of the army."

♦ The Alamist Queen ♦

Cenaya nodded to them. She wanted to speak, but no words would come.

Pointing toward a nearby archer, Haze lowered his arm. "Now!"

The archer released a multi-colored striped arrow into the sky above the grob army. Nate took a deep breath. The arrow exploded, showering the army with color.

"Al—Galo—Ominatta—Wslamet—Estella!" Nate chanted.

Bright rings of light appeared around Nate, Cenaya, and Ted. The sky filled with Efreet surrounded by their red mists and Druid warriors on the backs of the winged creatures.

"Now!" Nate ordered.

Nate, Cenaya, and Ted leaned forward together. The Efreet, Druids, and army waiting on the hillside descended on the grob army. With the rings of lights swirling rapidly around the trio, they propelled down the hill. Many grobs—including Meredith—dove out of the way. Those distracted by the attacking army didn't move in

♦ Scrolls of Zndaria ♦

time. The trio phased through them as if they were spirits. Passing through the courtyard, Cenaya held her breath. The hut's darkwood doors loomed in front of them. Before she needed to exhale, they rolled through the massive doors with ease.

"Stand up!" Nate commanded.

They all leaned backward at once, slowing their advance. When they were nearly standing, they came to a stop.

"Estella—Pesi!" Nate said.

The light rings disappeared. Cenaya and Ted released the staff. Nate planted it on the tile floor and leaned on it for support. He looked exhausted.

Surveying their surroundings, Cenaya debated their next move. Painted sculptures of countless varieties of snakes adorned the stone walls. An eerie chandelier resembling two dozen snakes ready to attack lit the entry.

"We need to find the dungeon. If Meredith left my people in the Troll Dungeon, my mother's

♦ The Alamist Queen ♦

probably in hers."

Green smoke billowed in a wooden staircase leading up. It dissipated, and Meredith stood before them. With her red hair flowing past her shoulders, smirking red lips, and emerald gown hiding the grotesque contours of her frog-like body, the witch looked exactly as Cenaya remembered her from the attack on her fort many years ago.

"Welcome, Princesssss."

Cenaya aimed an arrow at Meredith. "Give me my mother, or I will destroy you right now!"

"Sssssilly child." Meredith's smirk made Cenaya's stomach churn. "No need to threaten me. Jussssst like your pathetic army isssss no match for mine, you can't harm me," she sneered. "But, I'm not completely heartlessssss." She stepped to the side and gestured up the stairs. "I'll take you to your mother. Having both of you captive will buy me great power."

Cenaya stepped closer to Meredith. She didn't trust her at all. "What will stop me from killing you once I see my mother?"

"I asssssssure you," Meredith smirked, "many have tried. You are not fasssssster than my magic. My poissssson will reach you before your arrow isssss across the room. I will dissssssappear, and you'll be dead. But if you come willingly, you'll get to sssssee your mother again."

Nate and Ted started toward them.

"Don't listen to her!" Nate insisted. "It will be a trap."

Ted placed his hand on his sword's hilt. "We have ta take her down together."

Cenaya spoke over her shoulder. "I've waited over ten years to find my mother. If Meredith will take me to her, I'm willing to take the risk." She took a few more steps toward the Swamp Witch. She could almost touch her.

"Sssssmart choicccccce, child." Meredith tapped the floor with her serpent-shaped staff.

The tiles beneath Nate and Ted crumbled. The boys cried out in alarm and slipped through the floor.

Cenaya gasped. "What have you done?"

The tiles continued crumbling outwardly. The darkness below swallowed the brothers. A monstrous screech filled the air.

"I have no need for thossssse annoying boysssss." Meredith grabbed Cenaya by the arm.

Cenaya could no longer hear Nate or Ted calling for help.

Tightening her grip, Meredith pulled Cenaya onto the staircase. "Come with me now." Meredith's eyes tightened. "Or you'll join your friendsssss in their missssserable death."

Cenaya looked below. Could she sacrifice Nate and Ted even if Meredith was telling the truth?

"I'll save my friends and find my mother on my own," Cenaya spat. "And then I'm coming after you." She pushed Meredith away and jumped into the darkness.

Chapter Twenty-Three

THE LAIR

Cenaya fell into the darkness. Above her, Meredith cursed and tapped the floor with her staff. The crumbling tiles regenerated, sealing up the floor quicker than they'd fallen, stealing what little light Cenaya'd had. Glowing yellow streaks swished through the air around her, each releasing terrifying screeching. Was something alive down here? Pulling her knees toward her chest, Cenaya braced for a hard impact. Her feet hit something that bounced her back up slightly, causing her knees to buckle. She crumpled against the slick, scaly object and slid down, landing with a thud on something damp.

"Cenaya!" Ted whispered over the continued screeching. "Over here!"

The screeches made her cringe. The thrashing of feet around them made it worse. Something scraped her legs as she scrambled toward Ted's voice. Numerous glowing yellow eyes darted around above them.

Cenaya felt a foot. "Is that you, Ted?"

"It is. Move closer so yer out of the way."

Cenaya felt a damp wall of some sort and pressed her back against it. "Where's Nate? Are either of you hurt?"

"We're both fine," Nate said from the other side of Ted, "but we have to kill whatever that is before it gets us."

She pulled her bow forward. "Nate, do you still have your staff?"

"Of course, and Ted has his sword."

"On the count of three, Nate, you illuminate the cavern. Ted, you charge with your sword. I'll hit it with an arrow. We might be able to catch it off guard." Both Nate and Ted quietly agreed. They'd had the same thoughts. "Ready? One . . . Two . . ."

Something creaked above them on the other side of the cavern. Large doors split open. Sunlight spilled in. Cenaya stared at the creature that had broken their fall. Judging from the gasps next to her, Nate and Ted shared her shock.

An enormous hydra lumbered away from them toward the opening, pushing through the matted straw of the surrounding nest. Four thick legs supported a massive orb. Its nine heads weaved in all directions through the air, screeching continually. They nearly touched the top of the vast stone cavern. One of the heads snatched a red-spotted yellow frog a boot-length round from the moss-covered wall beside it. Another snapped at a striped insect as big as Cenaya's hand. Most of the heads screeched again. The sound of the battle ensuing outside drifted into the lair.

Ted pulled his sword. "We have to stop it before it reaches the army!" He didn't bother being quiet.

He rushed through the hydra's nest, past grassy mounds as tall as him. Oversized frogs sprang at him, gnashing their razor-sharp teeth. Nate rushed to help. A frog sunk its teeth into Ted's shoulder. He hit it on the top of its head. Cenaya readied an arrow. Numerous striped insects with sword-like noses buzzed around them.

Cenaya maneuvered for a shot that would miss Nate and Ted. Nate batted at the insects with his staff. One stung him on the leg. Ted smacked them away. They constantly moved into Cenaya's line of sight. She started around the edge of the nest.

Something cracked within the nest. The hydra stopped and started back toward them. Cenaya continued forward. She had to strike it before it got away. The brothers continued fighting off the frogs and insects. Some bounced off the mounds. Frogs and insects swarmed Cenaya. She swatted at them with her bow.

A grob grumbled from outside the lair. Several large stones rolled down a muddy incline and struck the hydra. Shrieking, it charged toward the open doors. More cracking sounded. The grass shook off the mounds, exposing the hydra's eggs.

Ted knocked away another frog and fought his way across the nest. The noise of the continued cracking filled the cavern. The hydra started up the incline. Small heads poked out of the eggs, letting out short, high-pitched screeches. Nate batted a frog at one of the baby hydras. The hydra snatched it into its mouth hungrily.

A head from one of the babies jutted out in front of Cenaya. She jumped back. The mother hydra neared the exit. More heads from the babies shot out, snapping at the trio, devouring insects and frogs.

They were too late. They couldn't stop the

hydra from reaching the army. If they followed it outside, they wouldn't find Cenaya's mother. A baby hydra snapped a frog off Ted. Jerking away, he swung his sword and lopped off the head. Before he could take another swing, two heads sprung out to replace the first.

"Nate!" Ted sheathed his sword and drew his crossbows, one in each hand. "We have ta get out of here!"

The now four-headed baby stomped at its egg, freeing its legs. It charged toward Ted. Cenaya released her arrow, striking the base of its necks. Greyness spread across the hydra. It froze in place, now a stone statue. Ted fired a bolt at another hydra, crystallizing its heads in ice.

"Falma—Ottsa—Omstrafa!" Nate struck a hydra with lightning. It shriveled away from him.

Nate and Ted worked their way toward Cenaya, batting critters away and dodging attacks of the hydra heads. Nate struck another hydra with lightning. More babies broke free from their eggs.

♦ Scrolls of Zndaria ♦

Cenaya glanced down an empty passageway beside her. "Ted! Nate! This way!"

The trio clambered out of the nest. Frogs and insects pursued them. Ted fired another bolt. Its blast of ice struck a frog and captured numerous more nearby. The mother hydra's muffled shriek came from outside the lair. The doors slammed together, once again engulfing them in darkness. High-pitched screeches, growly croaks, and buzzes surrounded them.

"Maloh—Octama!" Nate illuminated the cavern.

The baby hydras snatched at the frogs and insects. Their continued screeches sounded like cries for their mother. The trio hurried along the curving passageway, distancing themselves from the babies. The frogs and insects followed them. Whether in pursuit or retreat, Cenaya couldn't tell. It didn't matter.

The critters targeted the trio. It felt like their numbers continued to grow. Ted fired his crossbows, freezing several of them at once. Nate cast his lightning spell with his free hand and batted them away with his staff. Cenaya searched for their way out.

A sliver of light shone ahead of them. She rushed forward. The passage led up a muddy slope, ending at rocks sealing off the exit. The light came from a small opening she could barely reach her arm through. She glanced back. She could hear Nate, Ted, and the pests getting closer. She pulled two white arrows from her quiver. Nate and Ted rounded the corner.

Turning her bow on its side, she angled the two arrows away from each other. "Drop!" she shouted to the brothers. She released the arrows. Nate and Ted fell to the ground, fighting the few critters that joined them. As the arrows flew apart, strings formed between them. They struck opposite walls. A sticky web sprung up between them. The critters following them flew into the web, either getting stuck or bouncing off those already stuck.

The boys jumped up, slapping their attackers

to the ground. Ted froze them with a bolt.

Cenaya climbed down from the incline. "There's no getting out that way." She brushed her muddy hands against each other.

Ted holstered his crossbows. "Or that way." He nodded over his shoulder toward the baby hydras.

"What about that way?" Nate pointed to the ceiling that looked like a wooden floor. "I could blast it with lightning. Falma—Ottsa—"

"Wait." Cenaya put her hand over his. "If it causes a fire, we won't reach my mother in time." She pulled a green arrow from her quiver. "I can get us in." She shot the arrow at their feet. It flashed and began growing into a small oak tree. "Grab a branch, and protect your head."

The tree grew rapidly. They tucked themselves within the branches filling the passageway. The tree's crown pressed against the wooden floor. They huddled tighter. It crashed through, raining wood chips down on them. Carrying them higher, the tree rose into a small, musty room that looked like barracks. The branches expanded, pushing the iron beds and chests flat against the wall.

Ted jumped down, grabbing the single torch lighting the room just before it ignited the leaves. The crown cracked the room's ceiling, then stopped. Nate and Cenaya climbed down to join Ted.

Nate glanced into the hallway. "It's empty. Which way from here?"

Cenaya stepped out of the room and looked up and down the narrow halls. "Let's try . . ." She turned around. "Did you say my name?"

They both shook their heads.

"Cenaya."

She heard the faint voice again and this time, she recognized it. "This way! My mother is calling me!"

Chapter Twenty-Four

REUNION

Cenaya bolted down the simple wooden corridor. "Follow me. My mother is this way!"

Nate and Ted rushed to catch up.

"Cenaya," Ted called out, "we don't hear anything. What if it's just the Swamp Witch?"

"We have to stay alert." She peered around a corner. "I don't trust Meredith, but I know I hear my mother."

"Cenaya." Her mother's voice drifted through the hallway again.

Cenaya's heart leapt. She led them toward the voice, past eerie shadows cast by sparse torches along the walls to intersecting halls. In stark contrast, the simple wooden halls gave way to stone corridors lined with snake chandeliers. Their glowing eyes provided light. The corridors branched out, providing four different paths.

"Which way now?" Nate asked.

"I don't know." Cenaya glanced around. "Mother?" She spoke down the hallway as if speaking to Nate and Ted. If Cenaya could hear her calls, surely she could hear Cenaya's. "Mother?" *Please hear me, mother!*

"Cenaya, you're close to me."

"This way!" Cenaya rushed along the side hallway. She skidded to a stop at the top of stone steps. There were only eight steps, yet it felt like a bottomless pit. The sparse lighting of the barracks seemed bright compared to the light coming from below.

"Cenaya, my child! Come to me!"

"I hear it now!" Nate gripped his staff.

Ted pulled out his crossbows. "Expect anything ta happen."

At the bottom of the stairs, green marble statues of grobs stood next to a small wooden door. Cenaya stooped unnecessarily under the low ceiling.

"Mother?"

"I'm in here, my child!"

Tears sprang up in Cenaya's eyes. Her mother was alive! The iron knob refused to turn. She glanced around. A set of keys hung on a peg across the room. She grabbed them and tried the first two. Nothing. The third key creaked in the lock. The bolt clunked open.

"Wait, Cenaya!" Ted stepped in front of her. "This feels too easy. Are ya sure about this?"

"My mother is in there." She pushed Ted out of the way. "You guys stand guard. I'm going in."

Ted nodded at Nate. They closed in tightly behind her.

She turned the knob. The door creaked open. A sliver of light from a boarded-up window drew a line across the floor. Something shuffled in the corner.

Ted stopped at the door, both crossbows in hand. "I'll keep watch out here."

Nate stepped in behind Cenaya, lighting the room with his staff.

Cenaya gaped at a woman in shredded rags huddled on the floor next to an iron bunk. A thick chain hung between the bunk's frame and her ankle. Her faded purple hair hung over her face, nearly touching the platter on the floor with a few scraps of food in front of her. The woman looked up. A tear-shaped crystal pendant hung from her neck.

Cenaya rushed to her. "Mother!" She could barely speak the words. "Mother! I found you!" She flung her arms around her mother's neck. Tears flowed down her cheeks.

"My child!" Her mother's voice sounded like an angel. "I thought I heard you!"

Cenaya sat back to stare at her beautiful face. She'd dreamed of this moment so many times.

"I never gave up hope that you'd find me." Her mother brushed tears away from Cenaya's face. "Let's escape while we can."

"Of course, Mother!"

Cenaya pulled a black arrow from her quiver. She touched it to the chain link against her mother's ankle. Acid sizzled from the arrow, dissolving the chain on contact. Helping her mother toward the door, she couldn't stop smiling.

"You're free!" She swung her bow over her shoulder and took her mother by the elbow. "We'll get you to safety."

Ted met them at the door. "Follow me. We'll blast our way out the back of the barracks." They started across the dungeon.

"Wait." Her mother pulled weakly on her arm. "We need to go this way." She moved toward a simple door tucked in a crevice of the dingy room.

Nate and Ted exchanged questioning glances.

Ted stepped forward. "With all due respect, ma'am, how do we know where that will take us?"

Her mother continued limping forward with Cenaya at her side. "Like I heard my Cenaya from a distance, I've heard the guards speak of hidden corridors throughout the hut. One up there leads to freedom."

Cenaya glanced over her shoulder. "Let's trust her, Ted. My mother wouldn't lead us astray."

Ted bit his lip. "It don't feel right, Cenaya, but yer in command." He bumped Nate's shoulder. "Ya provide light behind me, and I'll lead the way."

They made their way up a handful of rickety wooden steps until they reached a second door. Matching the snake décor of the hut's hallways, the intricately carved design included a snake twisted to make the door handle. Ted held his crossbows ready and nodded. "Open it, Nate."

Holding his lit staff in front of him, Nate pushed open the heavy door and let Ted step past him.

"It's clear," Ted said. "Let's move fast."

Cenaya helped her mother into the room. It seemed to run the length of the hut. Nate pulled the door closed behind them. Bottles, jars, and crates of all shapes and sizes filled rows and rows of shelves.

"What is this place?" Cenaya gawked.

"Meredith's supply room," her mother said. "Impressive, isn't it? We'll be fine if we don't touch anything."

Cenaya scanned the shelves. The label on a small glass jar with long, sharp, bone-like items inside read *Vampire Teeth*. "How would one even get vampire teeth?" she spoke mostly to herself. She didn't want an answer. The tall glass bottle next to the teeth held colorful spirals and read *Unicorn Horns*. Cenaya's stomach churned. "That is horrific. How can someone be so wicked?"

"Her wickedness is more than you'll ever know." Her mother started walking a little faster. "We must hurry."

They followed Ted quickly through the room.

Cenaya couldn't pull her eyes away from the supplies. A round crystal bottle read *Leprechaun Lice*. A jar of dirty slime read *Brownie Mucus*. The disturbing bottles seemed endless. She read a few more labels: *Lightning Flies, Mermaid Scales, Cockatrice Eggs, Minotaur Hooves, Treeman Leaves,* and *Skeleton Rats*. Just when she thought it couldn't get worse, she spied a steel crate that read *Ogre Heads*. She shuddered and detested the Swamp Witch more than ever.

Ted stopped in front of them. "Stay behind me. We aren't alone."

Several swamp hounds snarled and growled at them from both ends of the supply room.

Ted fired at one, freezing it with a bolt.

"Falma—Ottsa—Omstrafa!" Nate shot lightning at one coming toward him.

It whimpered and flinched back.

Her mother pulled Cenaya between the brothers. "We can get out this way."

Ted froze a second hound. The glowing eyes of two more came out of the shelves behind the one

Nate had just struck. Cenaya's mother moved forward slowly, drawing Cenaya with her. The hounds sprang at Nate.

"Andia—Molas—Afay!" Catching one hound in the levitation spell, Nate flung it at the others, bowling them over.

Yelping, they rolled over each other until they crashed into a shelf. It toppled over, colliding with the shelf next to it, knocking it into the next one. One by one, every shelf in the room crashed to the ground, hitting another one. Ted froze a third hound, holstered his crossbow, and pulled his sword from his back.

"Get down!" He jumped in front of Cenaya and her mother.

Nate dove to them. A wall of ice sprayed out of Ted's sword, forming a shield. The shelves in front of them crashed to the ground. Shards of glass and wood bounced off the shield. Within a moment, all the shelves along that wall—and everything on them—lay on the ground in pieces.

Ted stood. The shield disappeared back into

♦ The Alamist Queen ♦

his sword. "Is anyone hurt?"

Before anyone could reply, a chorus started from within the rubble. A swarm of black bees buzzed upward. Thousands of tiny spiders scurried over the wreckage. Indescribable critters and creatures flew, crawled, or scampered toward them.

"Run!" her mother commanded. Holding Cenaya's hand tightly, she leapt over the rubble, dodging spilt liquids and broken glass while avoiding the pests. Nate and Ted followed them, firing at the creatures that chased them. Her mother ran straight toward a wall.

"Mother! We're trapped!" Scenes of her five-year-old self trying to escape the grobs flashed through her mind.

"Trust me!" Her mother jumped a stream of slime and reached the wall. She pressed a dark tile. A portion of the wall slid open, revealing a flight of stairs. Her mother started up the stairs.

Cenaya rushed to keep up. "Mother, how are you moving so quickly?" She could hear Nate and

Ted falling behind, battling the hordes of creatures below.

Her mother didn't look back. "There's no time to explain! Hurry!"

At the top of the stairs, Cenaya's mother touched another dark tile. The wall opened. She pulled Cenaya into a small room, then touched a different tile. The wall slammed shut behind them.

Cenaya pounded on the wall. "Mother! My friends are still down there. We have to help them!"

"They'll have to take care of themselves." Her mother's voice sounded less caring. "The Creator has sent help for us to escape, but only us."

Cenaya felt dizzy. "The Creator?"

"Yes, the Creator," a man's voice replied.

Cenaya turned to the voice. The man stepped out of the shadows. There in the Witch's Hut, sent by the Creator, stood her father.

Chapter Twenty-Five

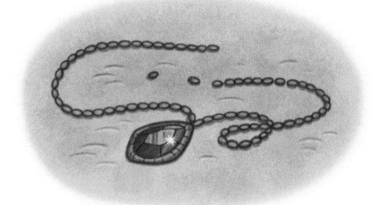

REDRESS

Cenaya's eyes moved between her father standing just out of the shadows to her mother placing items from a cluttered table in a leather pouch. They were all in the same room after all these years. She should be elated, yet she felt unsettled.

Shelves held jars and containers matching those in the witch's supply room. A cauldron hung over an open hearth. Several smaller versions of the snake chandelier from the hut's entrance lit the room. The Swamp Witch's staff rested against a pink crystal table in the corner that didn't match the décor. It reminded Cenaya of something from her childhood.

Cenaya looked back at her father. He watched her mother intently. He didn't smile. "Father?"

"Thank you for coming for us," her mother spoke without turning around. "I'm anxious to unite with the Creator."

"You vile creature!" Her father crossed the room in three strides.

Her mother whipped around from the table, nearly dropping a jar meant for her pouch.

"Natalia would never willingly join the Creator!" He grasped the crystal pendant and tore it from her neck.

Cenaya's hand flew to her mouth.

The woman Cenaya had believed to be her mother transformed before her eyes. Her frail, tall body shortened into a distorted, bulging swamp creature. Her faded purple hair became thick and red. It was all an illusion.

"You fool!" Meredith turned on her father. "Now ssssshe'll not go to the Creator ssssso eassssssily!"

Tears streamed down Cenaya's face. She'd felt so certain, so happy. "How dare you!" She trembled. "How dare you wear my mother's necklace! How dare you taint her image!"

"What game are you playing, witch?" He stepped between Meredith and Cenaya, his jaw tight. "I'm here at your promise to deliver the Alamist Queen. Where is Natalia?"

"You really are a fool! Your daughter'ssss the Alamisssst Queen you're delivering to the Creator." She tossed her curls. "Your precioussss Natalia died the night of the attack. Did the Creator not tell you?" she smirked. "We hid her people in the Troll Dungeon so when the princessss came of age we could make the elderssss take ussssss to the fairiessss to make her queen." Meredith leered at Cenaya. "Oncccccce you left Taycod, the Creator warned me you'd probably be coming for me. I almossssst gave up hope becaussssse you took ssssso long." She sneered. "But here we are, and it'sssss time to go."

Cenaya's father stepped backward. "I'm not taking either of you to the Creator."

Cenaya held her breath.

"But you mussssst!" Meredith screeched. "The Creator isssss expecting her. That'sssss why you're here."

"That is why he sent me." He pulled a dull grey arrow from his quiver—the one he'd received the first night Cenaya met the fletcher. "But your murderous treachery will not be rewarded."

"You can't harm me! You're bound by the Creator'sssss bidding."

"You're correct." He stepped backward beside Cenaya and handed her the arrow. "But I won't stop Cenaya from defending herself."

Meredith lunged for her staff. Cenaya swung her bow off her shoulder.

Meredith glared at Cenaya and her father.

"Now your daughter will sssssuffer the sssssame death her mother did!" She squeezed the staff just below the snake's head. Green smoke billowed from its mouth.

Cenaya released the arrow. Meeting the fumes as they neared Cenaya, the arrow began spinning. Each twist pulled the poisonous smoke into the shaft—and away from its target—until none remained.

Meredith gaped at the now dark green arrow. It lodged into her chest. "What have you done?" she shrieked. Her staff clattered to the floor. She stumbled toward them, gasping for breath. Dark streaks crept along her arms and neck. "You've ruined everything!" She dug her fingers into Cenaya's father's arm. "You've betrayed the Creator!"

"I shall face my consequences without regret." Her father pried Meredith's fingers off him and let her fall to the ground.

The darkness engulfed the Swamp Witch's face. Her body disintegrated. Cenaya shuddered.

Only a pile of dust beneath an emerald gown remained from the creature responsible for her mother's death.

She fell to her knees, sobbing. For over ten years, she'd dreamed of seeing her mother again. Now she knew that could never happen. "Mother's really gone." She looked at her father through blurry eyes. "How could I be so foolish? I put the army in danger to free someone who died a long time ago."

Her father knelt beside her and pulled her into an embrace. "You could only know if you attacked. Meredith had to be stopped, even if you couldn't free your mother." He released her and lifted her chin. "I wasn't there to save your mother from Meredith, but now, I can save you from the Creator."

Cenaya's eyes filled with tears again. Tears because of the tenderness in her father's gaze, for the love she felt from him.

He slipped a full quiver of arrows off his shoulder. "Eva prepared this for you when I told

♦ The Alamist Queen ♦

her you'd left. She suspected I'd see you again. She sends her love in a note that details the arrows uses." He pressed her mother's necklace into her hands, then caressed her tear-soaked cheek. "Honor your mother by becoming the Alamist Queen and using it to stop the Creator."

Cenaya gripped his hand. "He'll be furious!"

"I'll inform the Creator you slew Meredith in battle and escaped." His wet eyes looked down at her. The corners of his mouth turned up. "I'll accept his reaction proudly, knowing I kept you from his grasp."

"Once I'm queen, I'll use the Alamist to free you and your new family. We can be together again."

Her father kissed her forehead. "We will never be truly free unless the Creator is defeated. You have strong allies. You must use them."

A bang on the hidden door caused Cenaya to jump.

"Cenaya! Are you alright?" Nate yelled through the door. "Cenaya?" The banging continued.

"Nate, Ted!" She jumped up.

"I must leave, My Princess." He pulled her close and kissed her forehead once more, then rushed to the window. He looked back at her. "Alatava lashay!"

"Alatava lashay!" She called after him, returning their deepest expression of love.

Nate and Ted pounded again.

She hurried over, pressed a corner tile, and opened the door.

Nate and Ted rushed in, staff and crossbows ready to attack. Gashes covered both of their faces and Nate's arms. Their hair stuck out in a tangled mess. Colorful goo, fur, and blood clumped on their skin.

Ted lowered his crossbow. "Where's your mother?"

"She was never here. Meredith created an illusion using my mother's necklace." Cenaya lifted the pendant—the only thing she had left of her mother—and let it dangle from her hand. "The witch killed her the night she attacked our kingdom." She motioned to the pile of clothing and dust. "At least she died the same way. We need to get out of here." She wiped tears from her eyes, then tied the pendant around her neck. "It's time for me to become the Alamist Queen."

Chapter Twenty-Six

THE FAIRIES

Cenaya rushed out of the Witch's Hut. Nate and Ted followed right behind her. From within the courtyard they heard sounds of surrender: weapons clanging to the ground, shouts, and grunts. But which side won the battle? Stepping onto the battlefield, they stared in amazement. The massive hydra lay dead. Lopped off heads were strewn over the ground. She couldn't count the number of heads attached to the hydra.

Bloody bodies lay motionless. Deaths of the grob army highly outnumbered the attackers. Cenaya's people, the Druids, and Demon and his siblings surrounded the surviving grob army. With heads hung low, the enemy threw their weapons at their feet and slid them toward the victors. Ted's army rounded up grobs attempting to escape and collected the wounded. The Efreet searched the fallen, occasionally scooping up a soldier and flying behind the hydra.

Cenaya scanned the faces. Panic rose in her chest. She rushed to an Efreeti near her. "Where's Kathlyn and Haze?"

"Denya is caring for Haze." He nodded toward the hydra. "He was injured while slaying the beast. Kathlyn is with him."

Cenaya darted to them. Numerous soldiers lay on the ground, waiting for aid. Kneeling beside one, Kathlyn tenderly wiped blood from his upper body. Cenaya drew closer and stared at Haze's ashen face. Denya rapidly placed herbs over a gaping hole spewing blood on his side.

Cenaya dropped to her knees and grasped Haze's hand. She met Kathlyn's wet eyes. "Will he be alright?"

"He . . ." Kathlyn's words choked in her throat. She looked at Denya as tears streamed down her face.

"The hydra's venom is already coursing through his body, but the Druid healers can save him." Denya added another layer of herbs while speaking.

Cenaya jumped to her feet. "Then let's get him back there!"

"No. What—" Haze coughed up blood. "What of your mother?"

Cenaya cast her eyes down. Her heart hurt even more. "My mother is dead. She always was." Her eyes filled with tears. "The only good that came from this attack is that Meredith is dead."

"Then you must go become the queen." Haze gasped.

Nate and Ted came up behind her.

Nate touched her arm. "He's right, Cenaya. Ted and I are to take you to the fairies. Kathlyn and the Druids will care for Haze."

She looked from Nate and Ted to Haze. "But I can't just leave you and all of them like this." She gestured to the other wounded soldiers. "Not after you followed me into battle."

Denya secured a bandage around Haze's abdomen. "We'll be leaving shortly. The wounded will be properly cared for."

"We followed ya because we knew we needed ta stop the Creator and his Court." Ted turned her to face him. "We must get control of the Alamist."

Cenaya knew they were right. She watched Kathlyn lovingly wipe Haze's face. Her father had instructed her to use her allies. That meant she also had to trust them. The Druids and Denya would care for the wounded. She had to do her part. She whistled loudly. "Ted, gather your warriors and my people."

Ted rushed away, letting a high-pitched

whistle escape his own lips.

"Nate, get Demon." She knelt beside Kathlyn and squeezed her shoulders. She couldn't form the words to express her feelings.

Talia landed beside Cenaya with Prevesa on her back. Cenaya stood to meet them.

Prevesa slid off and rushed to embrace her. "Princess! I'm so glad you're safe." She wiped a tear from Cenaya's cheek. "Is it time for you to become our queen?"

Cenaya nodded, then smiled sadly. "I'm glad you're the one taking me to the fairies." She hugged her again and then turned to Haze and Kathlyn. "We'll join you on Eastern Island as soon as we can."

Flying low across the Clover Sea, Cenaya spotted the sparkling beach of her beloved island, the home she hadn't seen since she was a little girl. The peak of the Ismoala Mountain, blanketed by the Creator's gloomy mist, jutted out of the forest. Darkness from within the Rosewood Forest threw her back into her memories of a five-year-old fleeing a burning forest on a blanket of fairies.

"I've dreamed of bringing you home." Prevesa squeezed Cenaya's waist a little tighter, as if she'd read her thoughts. "But my heart aches that it's still occupied by the enemy."

Blinking back tears, Cenaya looked back at her handmaiden. "We'll drive them from our island and reclaim our home when the time is right."

She scanned the forest in front of her. The summer had been good to the edges not touched by the Creator's mist. The lush pink leaves stood out brilliantly against the deep-red bark. Shrubbery draped in berries and flowers hugged the trees. She led her people and Ted's army to the cover of tall trees wider than Talia. Oh, how she loved the Rosewood Forest.

Cenaya slid off Talia. "We will continue on foot." She secured Talia to a branch of one of the trees. The branch alone matched her in size. Her

♦ Scrolls of Zndaria ♦

people and Ted's army followed her lead. "Use caution. We could encounter the Creator's army at any moment."

Ted looped Lightning's reins around a sturdy branch, then turned to his men. "Foot soldiers." Several of his men stood at attention. "Remain with the animals. Stay on alert til we return."

"Yes, sir," they answered in unison.

Demon's bull head grunted at Nate and motioned toward the forest. Nate stroked his nose. "Yes, boy. You can come with us. The Druid Empress would want you to see Cenaya safely to the fairies."

"We must go now," Prevesa said. "There's no way to know if the Creator's army has spotted us. The sooner Cenaya becomes the queen, the better."

Nate swung up onto Demon's back. Prevesa darted into the forest toward the mist. Her recovery since the dungeon had proven spectacular. She led them up the steep mountainside with the speed and grace of someone twenty years younger. Reaching the rim, she dropped to her belly and motioned for them to join her.

In the valley below, withered leaves clung to the charcoaled bark of massive rosewood trees. Ten of them holding hands might reach around one of the trunks. The last time Cenaya saw this view, the fairies were carrying her to her father and away from her mother. Now, an evil army camp filled her treasured valley.

Cenaya shuddered, then turned to Nate and Ted. "The Ismoala Mountain," she said, pointing at the peak being circled by lava dragons, "holds the Alamist. Our fortress used to be at its base."

Prevesa placed her arms around Cenaya's shoulders. "The fairies are on this side of the mountain. We may be able to stay hidden, but we must be vigilant. Move from tree to tree."

Staying in the cover of the forest, they trekked down the mountainside, taking great effort to keep their footing sure. Prevesa often eyed the peak for a guide. As they neared the base of the mountain, the gloomy mist increased. They couldn't see the evil army, but they could hear them.

By the time they reached the base, the sun hung low in the sky. Prevesa stood within the forest, turning slightly in each direction. She walked toward a cluster of trees as if led by an unseen force. Stopping at each tree, she pressed her hand against its trunk and took a deep breath. At the fifth one, she turned to Cenaya with a smile.

"This is it." She reached for Cenaya's hand and pulled her closer. "When the Alamist's rightful heir touches the bark, entrance is allowed."

Cenaya reached out to the tree. The idea of ruling her people frightened her, but she was ready to take her place as the queen. She pressed her hand against the trunk. A portion of the bark pulled inward and slid open, revealing a hollowed center. Stairs carved into the wood led downward.

Cenaya looked back at her people and her

friends. "Shall we?"

Prevesa stepped in front of the group. "We must wait here for your triumphant return." She motioned gently for Cenaya to enter.

Cenaya swallowed hard. She hadn't realized she'd be doing this alone. She stepped inside the tree, and it closed behind her. She followed the stairs toward a faint glow. She could just see in front of her. Twisting around the trunk, she lost count of the steps. The light grew brighter, leading her to a low arch in the trunk. Stooping through the opening, she entered a lit, empty cavern formed by entwined glowing tree roots. Energy surged around her.

Something moved past the corner of her eye. Turning, she found herself face-to-face with dozens of fairies. No bigger than her thumb, the fairies' vibrant clothing resembled leaves and vines. They darted around her curiously, examining her armor, hair, and face. More fairies joined them until they filled half of the void. The sound of rushing wind swirled around her.

Gathering behind her, they gently pushed her forward.

They neared a rise along the far wall that created a wooden basin within the roots. Liquid dripped from overhead, sending ripples through the partially filled bowl. An elderly fairy fluttered up to her eyes. His tiny face looked torn between sadness and love. He bowed to Cenaya. Numerous fairies hoisted a human-sized goblet to her. Motioning to the bowl, the elderly fairy mimicked drinking.

Cenaya dipped the goblet in the basin, filling it with the clear liquid. She put the cup to her lips and drank freely. The cooling drink quenched a thirst she hadn't noticed until now. She swallowed the last drop. Pain seared throughout her body. Clutching her stomach, she cried out in agony. The goblet clanged to the floor. Her body shook. She struggled for breath and started falling. Forming a blanket, the fairies caught her gently and laid her on the ground. She writhed in pain.

She looked around at the fairies. Why weren't they helping her more? What had they done to her? A portal of light beamed down on her. The pain stopped. She rose into the light, but her body remained on the ground.

Chapter Twenty-Seven

THE ALAMIST QUEEN

The light encircled Cenaya. She looked below. The fairies hovered around her lifeless body. They'd killed her. She wanted to be angry, but the warmth surrounding her soothed her mind. She felt at peace. The light intensified. She shielded her eyes until it faded.

Cenaya found herself in a cloudy corridor. A gentle whiteness beckoned her forward. Numerous individuals walked ahead of her. Those further away disappeared from her sight.

A young man in ragged shorts with dreadlocked hair ran past her. "Mother?" He searched the faces of those he passed. "Mother?" he yelled ahead. "Mother? I'm here!"

A plump woman, one of the last Cenaya could see, turned around. A faded, colorful scarf tied around her hair matched her flowing skirt. She started back toward the boy. Her aged face smiled sadly. He rushed to her, wrapping her in a tight embrace. She caressed his cheek, and they continued on together.

Cenaya watched them vanish. Their tender exchange tugged at her. She walked quicker. Was her mother waiting for her? She neared the end of the corridor. Those in front of her passed through a cloudy wall without hesitating. She tried to follow but bounced off the wall. She stumbled backward. Trying again, she pressed her arm against the cloud. It felt solid.

A woman appeared in a light to her left. Her vibrant purple hair twisted in a bun highlighted her firm cheekbones. Her amethyst eyes sparkled with tears. "Cenaya!" She opened her arms. "My love!"

Cenaya rushed to her. The woman clutched her to her chest tightly. Warmth coursed through Cenaya's body.

"Mother?" Tears flowed freely down Cenaya's face. "Mother! Is it really you?"

The woman stroked Cenaya's hair. "Yes, my dearest! Oh, how I've longed to hold you again!"

"Mother!" Cenaya buried her face in her mother's shoulder. "Oh, Mother! I've missed you every day! Finally, we're together again!"

They stood in a silent embrace. Cenaya didn't track the time. She didn't want it to end.

Cenaya's mother pulled back to look into her eyes. "You've grown into an amazing young woman." She kissed her forehead. "You shall make a magnificent Alamist Queen."

"Queen? I don't understand. How can I be queen if I'm dead?"

Her mother stroked her cheek. A tear escaped

down her own. "Your soul is only temporarily parted from your body. The liquid from the fairies allowed you to come to me to receive the power of the Alamist and then return."

Fresh tears filled Cenaya's eyes. "But I just got you back. I want to stay."

Her mother took both of Cenaya's hands in her own. "I long to be with you again forever, but right now, Zndaria needs you. Your friends need you."

My friends? Since she'd arrived with her mother, Cenaya had only remembered her absence and the aching her embrace erased. Her mother's words reminded her of those waiting and relying on her: Nate, Kathlyn, her father. She looked to her mother with tear-filled eyes. "I don't want to lose you again."

"I'm always here for you, my love!" She pulled her close again. "We are connected by the Alamist, and we will be together again."

Cenaya soaked in the warmth of her embrace a moment longer. She took a deep breath and stood tall. She knew what she had to do. "How do I become the Alamist Queen? How do I use the Alamist?"

"You're already the queen." Her mother smiled lovingly. "The power of the Alamist passed to you when we first touched." She stroked Cenaya's hair. "As for using the Alamist, you'll know when you visit it." She wiped away a tear from Cenaya's face. "You now have the power to help save Zndaria. Use it wisely, my love!"

Cenaya felt their time together ending. She didn't want to say goodbye but couldn't turn her back on Zndaria. "I love you, Mother!" She buried her head in her mother's shoulder a final time. "I will make you proud!"

"I know you will, my darling!" Her mother squeezed her tightly. "You already have. You have all my love, my beautiful daughter." She kissed her forehead one more time. "Alatava lashay!"

Bright light flashed around them. Cenaya opened her eyes. She looked up at the fairies hovering above her. She could still feel the love of her mother's embrace and already missed her terribly. She sat up slowly.

The elder fairy appeared in front of her and bowed. "My queen, we are here to serve you."

"You speak?" Cenaya looked to them in awe.

"Only with you. When others hear wind through the forest, you will hear us." He bowed again. "It is time to rejoin your companions." He nodded to the fairies surrounding her. "But first, we shall bestow a gift upon you."

Fluttering behind her, the fairies helped her to her feet. The elder fairy moved toward the basin. The fairies nudged her forward, and she joined him. Several fairies untied her mother's necklace from her neck. In a flurry of color, they repaired the clasp, then filled the pendant with water from the basin. Replacing it around her neck, they fluttered around her in excitement. She felt a surge of energy. She could hear each of their excited exclamations.

"If you are ever in dire need," the elder fairy instructed, "utter, *cravretolisha*."

♦ Scrolls of Zndaria ♦

Cravretolisha. Cenaya thought the word at the same moment he spoke it. Her mother had said it many years ago just before the fairies came to their aid. She didn't recognize it at the time, but now it settled in her mind in such a way she didn't fear forgetting it.

"We are forever in your service." All the fairies bowed to her once more.

Moving from the cavern, they led her out of the tree. The light around her didn't fade as they made their way up the wooden stairs. The tree slid open, and she stepped outside.

Prevesa stood at once. She stared at Cenaya with her hand over her open mouth. Tears glistened in her eyes.

In the dimming evening light, Cenaya noticed a glow about her. She looked down. The liquid within her mother's pendant shimmered.

Prevesa bowed before Cenaya. Nate and Ted turned. Nate gasped softly, then both of them followed suit. One by one, the rest of Cenaya's people and Ted's army noticed Cenaya. One by one, they fell to their knees.

Cenaya watched the reaction in awe. She didn't feel any different but knew everything had changed. She had the duty to lead her people and wanted to make her mother proud. She now had the power to stop the Creator. She was the Alamist Queen.

♦ Scrolls of Zndaria ♦

Nate and Cenaya continue their adventure in the third scroll of the *Scrolls of Zndaria: The Rogue*.

Follow J.S. Jaeger on social media or join their newsletter on their website to receive updates and be one of the first to know when it's released.

Zndaria.com
Facebook.com/Zndaria
Twitter and Instagram: @zndariaseries

Short Scrolls of Zndaria

The *Short Scrolls of Zndaria* take readers deeper into the world of Zndaria by telling the stories of supporting characters from the main series. Starting with Nate's brother, Ted, and continuing with his sister, Denya, watch for future releases in this fun series of shorter stories that parallel the *Scrolls of Zndaria*.

AVAILABLE NOW ON AMAZON

COMING IN 2018

HEALING HANDS

About the Authors

Jerry and Stephanie Jaeger, J.S. Jaeger, love writing together to provide uplifting middle-grade fantasy for readers of all ages. Jerry has developed much of the storyline as he runs or bikes, furthering his fitness training and completing a full Ironman. Stephanie has discovered her favorite part of the writing/publishing process is visiting schools and loved sharing the Zndaria series with students in Japan and China. They're excited to draw readers further into the world of Zndaria as the series continues with Nate and Cenaya and the next three heroes.

Author's Note

Thank you for reading *The Alamist Queen*. We hope you enjoyed it. If you did, please consider leaving a review and spreading the word to your friends.

Thank you!

J.S. Jaeger

The *Scrolls of Zndaria* all began in *The Golden Wizard* with our first hero, Nathanial McGray.

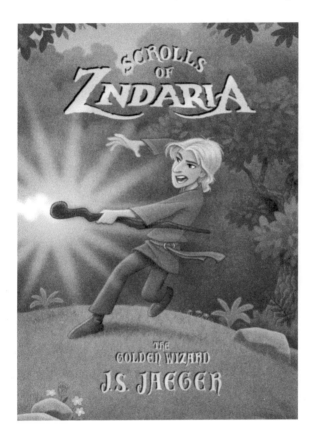

Scrolls of Zndaria
A magical read for all ages!

Reviews on *The Golden Wizard*

I can't tell you how much my 10 year old son enjoyed this book, he actually read it without being asked and talked about it all the time, for once he replaced all the gadgets with a book, it was fabulous to see. I would recommend this to all that are considering it!

Fuller, 5 stars (Amazon UK)

"Scrolls of Zndaria" is an excellent fantasy adventure story for teens and young adults. It has a great message of working hard to achieve one's goals. I highly recommend.

Ladyhawk, 5 stars (Amazon US)

What a fun and magical read! My ten-year-old and I both thoroughly enjoyed it. The writers did a good job of weaving an enchanting tale of magical proportions! I love stories that include moral lessons and this book does a good job of that.

Brandy D, 5 stars (Amazon US)

I bought this book for my granddaughter but decided to read the e-book also. I loved it!! Great story that keeps the reader on the edge of their seat until the end.

Amazon Customer, 5 stars (Amazon US)

Scrolls of Zndaria
A magical read for all ages!

Reviews on *The Dragon Slayer*

The Dragon Slayer by J.S. Jaeger is a middle grade fantasy short story of the Scrolls of Zndaria series. It follows Nathanial "Nate" McGray's brother Theodore "Ted" McGray on his journey to be Champion of the kingdom of Versii. It is a well written short story that takes us into a world of good vs evil.

Fee Roberts, 4 stars (Amazon US)

I'm not much of a fantasy reader but I bought this book for my granddaughter and thought I'd read it with her. I loved it!!! It had me hooked right away and I can't wait to read how the story ends.

Amazon Customer, 5 stars (Amazon US)